"Brett," Ellie w... **believe this!"**

"Why not?" he asked impatiently.

"Is there some reason why you've decided you need a wife? And since I'm—in place, so to speak, I might as well be it?"

He narrowed his eyes. "We're virtually living a phantom marriage right now. And the reason we got here was because we both have the same person's interests very much at heart. That has never changed."

Ellie was silent.

"As for the romantic side of things," Brett continued, "that's also 'in place,' wouldn't you say?"

"Romance is one thing, love is another, and that's what I need. It's been too long and hard a road to...compromise."

"Can you honestly say—" he sat forward "—that certain emotions the long, hard road froze are not clamoring for attention now? Eleven years is a long time to clamp down on wanting to... live and love."

Some of our bestselling writers are Australians!

Lindsay Armstrong...
Helen Bianchin...
Emma Darcy...
Miranda Lee...

Look out for their novels about the
Wonder of Down Under—
where spirited women win the hearts of
Australia's most eligible men.

THE AUSTRALIANS

He's big, he's brash, he's brazen—he's Australian!

Look out for the next Harlequin Presents® book
in THE AUSTRALIANS miniseries, coming soon!

Lindsay Armstrong

HIS CONVENIENT PROPOSAL

THE AUSTRALIANS

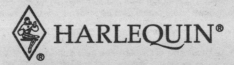

HARLEQUIN®

TORONTO • NEW YORK • LONDON
AMSTERDAM • PARIS • SYDNEY • HAMBURG
STOCKHOLM • ATHENS • TOKYO • MILAN • MADRID
PRAGUE • WARSAW • BUDAPEST • AUCKLAND

ISBN 0-373-12324-8

HIS CONVENIENT PROPOSAL

First North American Publication 2003.

Visit us at www.eHarlequin.com

Printed in U.S.A.

CHAPTER ONE

THE flight from Johannesburg to Sydney was long and tedious.

Therefore Brett Spencer didn't take offence when his business-class neighbour showed a tendency to be chatty. Of course, the fact that she was a sultry honey-blonde in her early twenties and wearing a scarlet skin-tight top with a plunging neckline that showed her amazing cleavage had nothing to do with his inclination to be chatty back.

By the time dinner was served, they were getting along famously. She knew he was a doctor on his way home to Australia from a stint in the Congo studying and treating tropical diseases. He knew she was a dancer who had just finished a stint with a revue at the Sun City resort in South Africa. He also knew that she danced topless but drew the line at performing bottomless.

'Very wise,' he commented, 'you could get sunstroke that way.'

Chantal eyed him suspiciously—she had true violet eyes set in an oval face and perfect creamy skin—then she giggled rather charmingly.

And over their marinated beef in a herb and mustard sauce served with a fine South African red, she poured out her life story. Born Kylie Jones, Chantal had refashioned herself in her pursuit of the only kind of fame she'd had the potential to achieve as she'd seen it. At the end of it, however, Brett had the strong impression that she might be a topless dancer with a fantastic figure

5

but she was also a shrewd survivor in the jungle of life and not a bad kid either.

After dinner they watched the in-flight movie, a comedy they both enjoyed, and they had a nightcap as the big jet flew on and on and the cabin grew quiet.

But far from feeling sleepy, although they'd extended their chairs, Chantal had other things on her mind apparently. So, bathed in their tiny cocoon of light, they chatted on quietly.

She told him that she had the offer of two jobs, both revues, one in Melbourne, one on the Gold Coast. Since Melbourne was her home town the sensible thing to do was to take that one, she felt, but she hadn't decided yet. Then she grew thoughtful and placed her hand lightly on his arm. He glanced at her shiny red nails then into her eyes, and guessed what was coming.

'Do you have a partner, Brett?'

He said after the briefest hesitation, 'At the moment, no.'

'I don't get the feeling you're a loner, somehow.' Her fingertips did a little tattoo on his arm.

'Not always,' he conceded. 'The Congo has its limitations in that line,' he added gravely.

'Why don't we get together? I *do* get the feeling you're my kind of man.'

'What kind is that?' he asked, and assured himself the only reason he was pursuing this conversation was because he was over thirty thousand feet above the earth hurtling through the night, trapped, in other words, on a long and boring flight.

'My kind of man?' Chantal said dreamily. 'There's a song that says it all, I've danced to it often enough—a man with a slow hand. A man who knows how to make a girl feel a million dollars. Tell me you're not that kind of man, Brett?'

He didn't agree or disagree. He said instead, 'I don't think you should go around making those judgements on face value, Chantal.'

'Oh, a girl can tell,' she assured him. ''Specially in my line of work. It isn't only looks and physique.' She raised herself on one elbow and her gorgeous eyes drifted over him. 'Not that they skimped on those when they were handing them out to you, but it's an aura, I guess. The way you talk, the way you smile, a sense of humour.' She shook her head. 'It's just there.'

For almost thirty seconds, as he stared into her eyes, Brett Spencer was tempted to prove her right—when they got to Sydney, naturally. One would have to be a block of wood, he reasoned, not to be tempted. But deep down he knew he couldn't further complicate his already complicated life.

'Chantal,' he said quietly, and covered her hand with his free one, 'thank you for the offer and don't think this is easy to do, but—'

'I'm not your kind of girl?' she supplied a little bitterly.

'On the contrary, you're the kind of girl to dream about.'

'The kind of girl you only think of in terms of sex?'

He paused and wondered, with a tinge of black humour, whether the flight was equipped with parachutes. He also praised his instincts that had seen him not divulge his surname. 'Look,' he said, 'I guess because I'm a bit older—'

'How much older?'

He shrugged. 'Thirty-five whereas you would be…twenty-one?'

She looked momentarily gratified. 'Twenty-four.'

'Even so, I've had eleven more years' experience of this business,' he said wryly. 'I think it's a good idea for two people to get to know each other before they take—that—plunge.'

'If this wasn't a plane I could show you different, Brett,' she said huskily. 'You have to start somewhere.'

How right you are, Kylie Jones—damn! Brett thought. I must be mad.

'So,' she continued, 'let's be honest. I'm not and never could be the right girl for you except as a one-night stand?'

'Let's put it another way—I'm not and never could be the right man for you.'

'How do you like your women, then? All intellectual and upper crust? I can tell by the way you talk you're both intellectual and upper crust yourself.'

'It's nothing to do with that. Chantal, if I'm not the right man for you, that doesn't mean to say there isn't a Mr Right out there—you're lovely enough and nice enough. Just—' he hesitated '—take it a bit slower. But for what it's worth—' he smiled down at her '—here's looking at you, kid!'

She fell asleep eventually but he didn't. Perhaps because his life was about to change drastically, he mused. He was going home for the first time in five years. Back to civilization to ride a desk, and he wasn't at all sure about it. Yes, he knew he needed a break. Not only that but he had papers to write and a new disease to move on to. And it wasn't that he didn't enjoy civilization but for how long he'd be able to resist the call of the wild—the call to work amongst people who desperately needed help—was another matter.

Then there was Elvira Madigan. His best friend's girl-friend whom he'd rescued and set up in his own home, a girl it had several times occurred to him to marry but for all the wrong reasons—well, almost all…

CHAPTER TWO

THE first note on the fridge door said:

Dear Mum
Just want 2 let u know I'm not blind. I can tell there's
a new man in your life by the amount of time u spend
fiddling with your hair—I hope he's a better choice
than the last one. But worse than that, I can c there's
not a bloody (note I do not use the F word) thing to
eat in this fridge!!! Your loving son, Simon.

The second note in a more mature hand read:

Simon, on the contrary, this fridge is full of things to
eat. True, there are no frozen, instant, microwavable
meals, if that's what you're on about, but that's be-
cause they're not good for you on account of their
high fat, sodium etc., etc., content. By the way, the B
word is no more acceptable than the F word, so please
discontinue its use.
Love, Mum.

A pencil drawing of a freckle-faced boy crying croc-
odile tears adorned the third note:

Mum, I'm only 10! I haven't had the time 2 learn 2
cook yet! So what's wrong with a frozen pizza now

and then? Just 4 when I get desperate? Other kids eat them all the time and they don't seem 2 be dying off because of them. Also, don't forget u r a working mum and I'm your only son. Simon—growing boys of the world unite against hunger!

The last note was the longest:

Son, blackmail will get you nowhere. And what you're implying is not true. I cook you two nutritious meals a day and I exhaust myself creating imaginative, filling and delicious lunches for you to take to school. So there is no need for you to add cooking to your array of skills at present. But if between meals is the problem, I'm quite sure you're old enough to make a sandwich (or 6!) out of the cold meat, salad items, cheese and the like that this fridge holds in abundance. And if you're really dying to drive the microwave, at this point in time for example, there's some chicken casserole left over from last night that only needs reheating. Mum—overworked, undervalued mothers of the world unite!

There was a pencil sketch at the bottom of the note of a woman with six hands filled with pots and pans, a broom, an iron and with her hair pinned up with clothes pegs.

It was a pleasant kitchen that the fridge-cum-message-board stood in. It had always been a pleasant room with terracotta tiles on the floor and a view of the garden, but there were added touches Brett Spencer did not remember as he turned away from the fridge with a lingering smile.

New yellow curtains with white daisies, pots of basil, thyme and parsley on the window sill, colourful jars of preserved chillies and other evidence of a cook who took her cooking seriously; a set of black-handled knives from carving through to chopping and paring in wooden block holder, a food processor, a garlic press, a bowl of lemons and a full spice rack.

At one end of the room was a round table with four ladder-back chairs. The surface of the table was cluttered with books, magazines, a fruit basket, a cricket ball and two baseball caps.

Then the back door opened precipitously and a boy pelted into the kitchen. He pulled up abruptly as he saw Brett.

'Who are you?'

A little jolt of recognition ran through Brett. There was no doubting whose son the child was…

'You must be Simon,' he said lightly as the fair, freckled boy slung his school bag onto the table causing the cricket ball to roll off. 'I'm Brett. I've come to see your mum.'

'Gosh!' Simon eyed him alertly, then picked up the ball and rolled the seam between his fingers. 'Don't tell me she's got it right at last.'

'Got it right?'

'She has awful taste in men,' Simon confided. 'But you look pretty normal and if that's your car in the drive, it's *real* cool!'

'Uh—it is—but what makes you say she has awful taste in men?'

'Well, the last one had this thing about getting back to nature. He was forever taking us on hikes and orien-

teering expeditions and he was into birds and bush
tucker and he didn't believe in television and he never
stopped trying to teach me knots and survival skills—I
tell you, I was absolutely worn out when she finally saw
the light! You're not a back-to-nature-freak, are you?'
he asked warily. 'I mean, you look OK, but I guess you
can't tell until you know a person.'

'No, I'm not, but—'

'Then there was the artist,' Simon went on blithely,
but screwed up his face. 'He didn't know one end of a
cricket bat from the other and he was always putting her
down.'

'Putting her down?'

'Mum likes her art conventional. He used to say she
had the artistic appreciation of a hen. I used to tell her
that a hen with a paintbrush could probably come up
with better art than *he* could.'

'Well done, but—'

'You sure you're not an artist in disguise?' Simon
eyed his khaki trousers and blue shirt.

'Quite sure,' Brett said wryly. 'And I happen to like
my art conventional.'

'Then—' Simon rolled his blue eyes '—there was the
father figure. Had to be the worst of all!'

'Why was that?'

'He was always trying to help me with my homework;
he was mad about playing Scrabble and chess; he used
to make up these general knowledge quizzes.' Simon
shook his head wearily.

'Worse than the back-to-nature freak?' Brett enquired
gravely.

'Yes. He had no sense of humour!'

'That is tough to live with,' Brett agreed.

'More so if you have a mum who can be a little wacky

at times. But he just didn't get it so she used to try and be all serious. I love my mum the wacky way she is.'

'Were there any that you liked at all?'

Simon chewed his lip, then looked as mischievous as only a freckled, ten-year-old boy could. 'There was one I didn't mind. Not that I liked him 'xactly, but he used to slip me five bucks and tell me to get lost for a while.'

'I see. Incidentally you haven't got that flipper quite right—can I show you?'

Simon handed over the cricket ball and Brett positioned it in his hand with his fingers on the seam and went through the bowling action in slow motion. 'See? You need to flip your wrist over like this so it comes out of the back of your hand.'

'You…like cricket?' Simon asked with an awestruck look in his eyes. 'More than Scrabble and chess?'

'More than most things. So. You assumed I was the new man in your mum's life?'

Simon shrugged. 'Who else would you be? She's got a new hairstyle and she painted her nails the other day. Isn't that what girls do?'

'They…yes, probably,' Brett Spencer murmured.

'And you're here in the kitchen so I guess she told you to let yourself in—hey! You're not a teacher, are you?'

'No. And I am in the kitchen.' Brett put the ball back on the table and they both turned as a woman came in through the back door.

'Simon, sorry I'm late,' she said breathlessly. 'Did you get a lift home? I guess that's got to account for the strange car. Who—?' She stopped dead as her gaze fell on Brett Spencer, and dropped her purse.

It was five years since he'd last seen Ellie Madigan, Brett Spencer mused. Five years that had treated her kindly—either that or reaching thirty had brought together all her potential. Gone was the naive, unsure-of-herself girl his friend Tom King had introduced him to eleven years ago. Gone was the sick, desperate girl of not much later. Gone was the rather limp, colourless mother of a particularly energetic five-year-old she'd been on that last occasion.

In fact, until she'd frozen to the spot, she'd radiated energy. There'd been a spring in her step and a wry little smile on her lips. And she certainly wasn't colourless. Her brown curly hair shone and was cut in an attractive short bob, her skin was smooth and fresh, her hazel eyes with their little flecks of gold were clear and expressive, and her slender figure beneath a short yellow skirt and a white stretch T-shirt made you doubt she could be the mother of a ten-year-old.

'You!' she said at last. 'I didn't know...I didn't expect...' She stopped and bent to pick up her purse.

'My fault, I should have let you know, Ellie,' Brett said. 'I hope you don't mind me letting myself in?'

'Uh—well, it is your house.' She swallowed visibly. 'So you and Simon have got to know each other?'

'I sussed out that he was the new man in your life—what do you mean it's his house?' Simon asked, turning to stare at Brett suspiciously.

'We hadn't got around to that yet,' Brett murmured. 'Simon, I'm Brett Spencer. We have met before but you were only five.'

Simon stared, then his mouth fell open as dawning comprehension came to him. 'You mean you were my dad's best friend? Jeez—'

'Simon!' Ellie murmured warningly.

'But this is great, mon!' Simon turned to his mother enthusiastically. 'Not only that but this guy likes his art conventional, he's not into the birds and the bees, he doesn't mind a bit of wackiness—what more could you want?'

Ellie had to smile although weakly. 'Simon—'

'And he can bowl flippers! It just gets better! Though why you couldn't tell me who he was I'll never know. Um…guess what? I'll leave you two alone for a while.' Simon grinned wickedly. 'And it won't even cost you a cent,' he added to Brett.

He took an apple from the fruit bowl, put one of the baseball caps on backwards, picked up his cricket ball and sauntered out.

'Won't cost you a cent?' Ellie said dazedly as she sank down into a ladder-back chair. 'What does that mean?'

'One of your ex…one of the men in your life used to tip him five dollars to make himself scarce.'

The colour rose from the base of her throat, he noted, and spread to the clear fresh skin of her cheeks as she said, 'You're joking.'

'Not unless Simon is given to making things up.'

'Simon,' she said bitterly, 'is the most devastatingly honest person I know. Oh, no!' She got even hotter. 'Conventional art, the birds and the bees, wacky—he told you about them *all*?'

'He ran through four of them.'

'But why? How come you were discussing me like that?'

Brett grimaced. 'He assumed because you had a new hairstyle there was a new man in your life, and because he found me in the kitchen and because I said I'd come to see you—that I was it.'

'That still doesn't explain…' Her eyes were wide and incredulous.

'It would appear—' Brett chose his words with care '—that he hasn't entirely approved of your choice of men.'

'Do you think I don't know that?' Ellie's voice rose. 'I chose them all because I thought they could enhance a facet of his life I was unable to but he...' She broke off and breathed heavily. 'He was so sickeningly polite and determinedly unimpressed it was just awful.'

'Perhaps you should have chosen them for yourself?' Brett suggested.

'Well, obviously I liked them, or I thought I did, until Simon got to work on them.'

'Someone with a good working knowledge of cricket might have been a better bet.'

Ellie propped her chin in her hands. 'What are you here for, Brett?'

He pulled out a chair and sat down opposite her. 'The time has come to talk of many things—wouldn't you say, Ellie?'

'"Shoes and ships and sealing wax"...do you want your house back?'

Brett Spencer was thirty-five and six feet two. He had grey eyes, dark hair, a rather hard mouth when he wasn't smiling and the aura of a man who knew what he wanted—and got it. The one thing he had never wanted was his best friend's girlfriend, Ellie Madigan...

'No.' He fingered the blue shadows on his jaw. 'Unless you have plans to marry someone and move out?'

Ellie smiled bleakly. 'No. I would have thought that was obvious.'

'What about the new man?'

'Who said there was a new—?' She paused and her gaze refocused on the other end of the kitchen. 'You've been reading the notes on the fridge!'

He nodded wryly and looked at her neatly painted nails, a soft pretty pink. 'Simon was certain of it.'

Ellie muttered something beneath her breath. 'I have no plans to marry him.'

'But you're stepping out with him?'

'I...' She reddened again, then tossed her head. 'If you call going to lunch and...oh, damn! I nearly forgot, I've asked him to dinner.'

'Brave of you,' he commented, and started to laugh.

'It's not funny!' But despite her indignation a hidden tremor ran through Ellie—Brett Spencer was devastatingly attractive when he was genuinely amused.

'Storming the Bastille might be child's play compared to running the gauntlet of Simon for any of your suitors, Ellie. But I'll be here to lend a hand.'

'You?' Her eyes widened. 'You intend to stay here?'

'I do.' He shrugged.

'For how long?'

'I've moved back to Australia.'

Hazel eyes met grey ones. 'But...?' Ellie all but whispered and swallowed visibly.

'I'm quite happy to share my house with you and Simon.'

'So...' Ellie cleared her throat. 'So what's the deal?'

'The only deal is that we don't have to rush in—or out—of anything at the moment.'

Ellie absorbed this. 'Why have you moved back to Australia? You seemed to be content to spend most of the last ten years fighting disease in Africa.'

Brett moved his shoulders. 'Perhaps I'm tired of Africa. Anyway, I've been offered a grant to set up a laboratory here to study Ross River Fever.'

Ellie blinked. Ross River Fever, a flu-like mosquito-borne virus, took its name from the river in Townsville,

North Queensland, where it had first been identified. 'That's…interesting,' she said lamely.

'It is to me,' he replied gravely. 'I don't expect you to be jumping over the moon about it.'

Ellie grimaced. 'Sorry. I'm still in shock, I think. Why—didn't it cross your mind to give me some warning of all this, Brett?'

'It did but I didn't want to worry you unnecessarily.'

'Oh.'

'You're looking well, Ellie,' he said then.

Don't do it to me, Ellie prayed as his gaze swept over her. Don't subject me to a summing up on a scale of one to ten as a woman, Brett, I *know* I've never registered on your scale either mentally or physically!

But he did it briefly despite her prayers, and you would have had to be a block of wood not to be affected, she knew all too well. Because Brett Spencer might be a dedicated doctor with an impressive history of research into tropical diseases behind him, but that didn't mean he couldn't look at you in a certain way that made you go weak at the knees. That didn't blind you to the awesome possibilities of being found attractive by this tall, sometimes arrogant but rather divinely proportioned man with his worldly grey eyes.

In fact, she picked up a magazine and stood it on the table in front of her just in case her nipples decided to misbehave themselves, and she threatened to shoot herself if she blushed.

'Thanks, I feel pretty good,' she said brightly.

'So, other than on the man front, life is treating you well?'

A fighting little glint lit her eyes for a moment at the 'man front' bit but she decided to ignore it. 'Very well! I finally got my degree in speech therapy and I work part-time at a local clinic, mainly with children. I love it.' Genuine enthusiasm replaced the fighting glint in her eyes.

'Would I be wrong in assuming Simon—he's so like Tom, isn't he?—is also above-average bright?'

Ellie let the magazine fall. 'You wouldn't. He absorbs knowledge like blotting paper. I…it…that's why I sometimes feel I need to broaden his scope.'

'Then it's a good thing I came home,' Brett said lightly and stood up. 'Would you mind if I unpacked and took a shower? I've been travelling for days and I need a shave.'

'Not at all, if you'd just give me a few moments to clear your bedroom.'

He raised an eyebrow at her. 'You've had other men in my bedroom, Ellie?'

'I have not,' she denied hotly. 'My market gear is in there, that's all.'

'Market gear?'

'I make kites and sell them at the local markets—I have a stall one Sunday a month, remember? It was a project I started so that one day I'd be able to repay you. All the proceeds,' she went on stiffly, 'are in a bank account that's become quite substantial over the years. It's all yours.'

'My dear Ellie,' Brett Spencer said with just the right mix of quizzical affection he might have accorded a dog that had brought him a bone, 'you didn't have to do that. Keep it as a nest egg.'

An hour later, Ellie closed herself into her bedroom and leant back against the door, not sure whom she was most furious with: herself, Brett Spencer or Simon.

She'd cleared Brett's bedroom and she'd supplied him

with a pink razor when he'd discovered that he'd picked up the wrong hand luggage from the plane. She'd listened with one ear as he'd called the airline and told them what had happened, including the possibility that the person he'd sat next to on the flight from Johannesburg might have been the one to pick up the wrong bag in Sydney.

She'd tried to contact the man she'd invited to dinner to cancel it but she hadn't been able to reach him, so she'd got dinner under way although with definite trepidation, and she now had about an hour to herself.

And as she wandered over to her bedroom window she could see Brett bowling flippers to Simon.

Brett's house had a lovely garden and a swimming pool. In fact it was a lovely house: brick, old, solid and mellow with bay windows and flourishing creepers on the walls, a red tiled roof. The rooms were large and high-ceilinged, some of the furnishings a little faded now, but to Ellie's mind that only gave it the patina of a much-lived-in home. And as well as a lawn large enough to play cricket on, there was a shady paved terrace guarded by two stone lions that overlooked the pool, and suited the subtropical climate of Brisbane perfectly—she used it a lot, they often ate outside.

Not that she was really furious with Simon, she thought ruefully as she turned away from the window. Imparting the details of her love life, such as it was, to a complete stranger was…well, just Simon, a son she adored.

Brett Spencer was another matter. So was her reaction to him.

Her mind slipped down the years to her earlier reactions to him…

* * *

She'd met Tom King at university when she was eighteen and he was twenty-two, a civil engineering student, dashing and to-die-for handsome... He'd had his own apartment, a car, he'd played polo and he'd been wonderful to be with. Especially for a girl who had grown up in a repressive home life with a jealous stepmother after her own mother had died. Tom took life so differently, she'd often thought. There had been none of the undercurrents of her home life, none of the suspicions, none of the rules and regulations. It had been heady and intoxicating.

He'd been gregarious with a large circle of friends, but the friend he'd seemed to treasure most and even look up to had been Brett Spencer, a little older and a doctor. Brett Spencer, a man who'd tended to make you stop in your tracks and think, Wow!—even when you'd been in love with another man. Nor had it been so hard to put your finger on why he'd had that effect.

At twenty-four Brett had already had that air of knowing what he wanted and getting it; he'd been enigmatic, he'd played polo brilliantly but he'd obviously been an academic, he'd been laconic—at times he'd even been curt—but when that brilliant smile had crinkled his face and lit up his grey eyes, women had simply keeled over.

And gradually Ellie had discovered why Tom had thought so much of Brett. Their families had been close when they'd been children, they'd been to the same schools, they'd played on the same polo team and at thirteen, when Tom's parents had died in a ski-lift tragedy, he'd gone to live with the Spencer family.

But she herself had never felt quite at ease with Brett Spencer. Not that he'd ever said anything, but she'd sometimes got the depressing feeling that he hadn't taken her seriously, that he'd seen her as a passing romance for Tom, a sowing of his wild oats. To be honest, she'd sometimes wondered about this herself. She hadn't fallen naturally into Tom's crowd. She'd been having to put herself through university via a series of part-time jobs, she'd certainly not been as sophisticated as many of the girls in the crowd and she'd sometimes lacked confidence in herself.

And, in hindsight, she was able to identify that her reluctance to become Tom's lover, not that she hadn't wanted to, had led him to pursue her all the more.

By the time she was nineteen and had known him for six months, she'd succumbed to the pressure and surrendered her virginity to Tom King and life had been wonderful. A month later life had done an about turn and hit her hard. Tom had been killed in a freak polo accident and a few short weeks after it she'd discovered the contraception she'd used had failed and she'd been pregnant. So, where to turn? She'd had no intention of living with her stepmother's disapproval on top of all the other things they hadn't seen eye to eye about.

Then fate had taken a hand. Morning sickness had kicked in with a vengeance and she'd been standing on a pavement in the middle of Brisbane, clinging onto a parking meter feeling not only sick but dizzy and as if she'd been about to faint, when Brett Spencer had walked past, recognized her and come to her assistance. And after he'd restored her, it hadn't taken him long to prise out of her what the problem had been. His expression, when she'd told him, had said it all—a kind of weary cynicism but not a great deal of surprise that she should have got herself into this situation.

But almost immediately, he'd got practical. He'd told her that he had settled Tom's affairs but the hope of any assistance from his estate as the mother of Tom's child would not be forthcoming. Tom's lifestyle had eaten away his inheritance from his parents. In fact, all his assets had either been in hock or had had to be sold to meet his debts.

What Brett had then proposed, however, had surprised the life out of Ellie. He'd offered her a home and financial assistance—he'd offered her and her baby security with no strings attached while she'd found her feet again. It had been something of a mystery to Ellie why, at the time, she'd found the prospect oddly chilling.

Of course, she'd knocked the whole thing back at first for so many reasons, not least how little they'd known each other, but Brett Spencer had had other ideas. And on top of what had been turning out to be a difficult pregnancy, he'd finally worn her down. He'd even held her hand, as a doctor, when her son Simon had been born…

Ellie came back to the present. The amazing thing, of course, was that eleven years down the track she was still here.

For her part those eleven years had passed so fast, she sometimes had to pinch herself. But why had Brett been content to let the situation last for so long?

She ran a bath, poured in some salts and got into it absently. How many times had she wondered this down the years?

She squeezed the flannel over her breasts and watched the bubbles slide down her skin. Truth to tell, the only way to cope with providing Simon and herself with a stable, happy life in the circumstances had been to bury this question at the bottom of her mind.

But she had to ask herself now why *she* hadn't made a break years ago. Before they'd got too settled in Brett's lovely old Balmoral home with its views of the Brisbane River?

Because it had been so easy to float along with the tide, she answered herself. Brett had inherited the house from his parents. He might spend large chunks of his life away from it but he'd never planned to dispose of it so, it was there, he'd told her when he'd so efficiently reorganised her life for her, and it was silly for her not to use it. And it had also been home to Tom.

'Only until I get on my feet,' she'd warned, as if, she now marvelled, he'd suggested something faintly distasteful or illegal.

He'd shrugged and replied, 'Whatever.'

So she'd moved into the house and Brett had maintained his city apartment. When Simon had been nine months old, he'd left on the first of his overseas projects and been away for a year, and from that time on his trips home had been brief and for the past five years he hadn't come home at all.

Her contact with him had been via his solicitor, Gemma Arden, who in time had become a friend. Brett had arranged for Ellie to have an allowance and had insisted on meeting all costs of the upkeep of the house. He'd even provided her with a small car.

So much of this had gone against the grain with Ellie, she'd had a hard time rationalizing it. But by the time the effects of a complicated pregnancy and a protracted birth had worn off, it had all been well in place. Then, her limited prospects of taking care of herself and Simon had become apparent. She'd been forced to cut short her degree so she'd had no qualifications and, even with what part-time work she would have been able to get and a single mother's pension, child-minding would have cut into any wages drastically.

And although Simon was as fit and healthy as they came now, he'd not had a trouble-free run as an infant. Lactose intolerance, frequent ear infections that had eventually required grommets, and adenoid problems had plagued his early years. She'd often stopped to wonder wearily in those years how single, working mothers could possibly cope.

Some justification for the largesse Brett had showered on her had come, obviously, from the fact that Simon was his best friend's child—perhaps even more than a best friend, almost a younger brother. The other thing, although Ellie didn't see it as justification but it was a factor to be considered, she supposed: Brett was wealthy. There was a brewing empire in the family background and he was a shareholder.

But even though she'd gone with the flow, so to speak, she'd tried to be as frugal as possible. She'd never exceeded her allowance, she'd insisted on it being cut when she'd started earning money, and she'd hit on the kite-making as a way of paying something of it back.

The other thing she'd done was take extremely good care of his house. In fact she'd come to love it as if it were her own. She'd also discovered she had green fingers and his garden now looked better than it had ever done. And the house and garden had provided her with occupational therapy down the years.

Some help had come her way from her father until he'd been transferred interstate. What had happened to his only daughter might have perplexed and disturbed him but he'd adored Simon. And he wrote to Simon regularly and every year he paid for Ellie and Simon to spend a holiday with them.

But there was no doubt she'd needed some occupational therapy while she'd grappled with child-bearing and -rearing on top of losing Tom, and a life that had been turning out quite different from her expectations.

Thirty now, a single mother, essentially dateless—apart from the few men she'd hoped Simon might relate to—and desperate, she thought ruefully.

She sat up, reached for her loofah and started washing herself vigorously but it was no good. The underlying reason she was still in Brett's home refused to be submerged beneath a lather of soap and the scrape of a loofah. It was still the perfect solution to her life, wasn't it?

CHAPTER THREE

'I DON'T get this,' Simon said stubbornly, half an hour later. 'Now Brett's come home, why do you need a date with another man?'

'Simon, just set the table, please,' Ellie responded. She glanced at her watch and then through the open door to the dining room. 'We've only got about ten minutes.'

Simon stood his ground. 'Who is this bloke?'

Ellie drew a deep breath. 'His name is William Brooke. He's a musician and I met him when he bought one of my kites—you remember the racing car one you helped me to make? Well, he really liked it and bought it for his nephew. We got talking and he asked me to have lunch with him. That's all.'

'What kind of a musician?' Simon asked with palpable foreboding.

'He…he's a concert violinist.'

'Mum! So that's what it's all about! You want me to start playing the violin—yuk! Martie Webster has to practise for an hour a day and it sounds like…it sounds as if he's strangling *cats*.'

Ellie ran her fingers through her hair and smoothed the long indigo cotton-knit dress she'd changed into. She said, 'Musical appreciation is something that can enhance your life. I've always regretted not learning to play an instrument when I was a kid and I didn't want you to grow up with the same regret. So—'

'You're the one who banned the bongo drums Grandad sent me for Christmas!'

28

'That was different, that wasn't music and I was in imminent danger of going deaf!' Ellie picked up a ladle and stirred the soup she was tending.

'Mum, I'm quite happy the way I am! You really don't have to—'

'Simon,' Ellie spoke rapidly, 'this has turned out to be a difficult day for me. I tried to put William Brooke off but he's not answering his phone, therefore I can do nothing but expect him for dinner, so you will set the table because I'm telling you to, and because I'm your mum I'm entitled to tell you to do things and because you're my son you're entitled to listen to me. OK? And I'll tell you something else—you'll behave yourself tonight because if you don't I'll have a conniption—you wouldn't like that, would you?'

Simon grinned. 'The same kind of conniption you had when that guy reversed into you and tried to tell you it was your fault?'

'Oh, *much* worse!' She banged the ladle on the counter, then inspected herself for soup splashes.

'All right, calm down, Mum. I'll set the table.'

'What about behaving yourself?'

'I'm quite happy to behave myself so long as you understand that you don't need to bring home all sorts of blokes to enhance my life.' He walked through to the dining room.

Ellie picked up the ladle and turned to see that Brett Spencer had come into the kitchen via the back door. She couldn't doubt, from the amusement of his expression, that he'd heard it all.

'Don't say a word!' she warned him darkly.

'OK.' He put a box on the table and drew a chilled bottle of wine from it. 'Your wine cellar appears to be non-existent so I nipped out to the bottle shop.'

He came over to the counter, opened a drawer and pulled out a corkscrew. Two minutes later he handed her a glass of wine and poured a beer for himself.

Ellie inspected the pale gold liquid in the crystal glass, then closed her eyes and sipped it gratefully. 'You couldn't—' she stirred the soup gently '—also arrange to have me wafted to…to Africa or the moon for this evening?'

He was standing next to her, leaning against the counter. He was still looking amused. He'd changed, he'd shaved and there was something oddly reassuring about him mixed in with something that sent a frisson tiptoeing down her spine.

'Sorry, no, but it may not be as bad as you think. I don't suppose there can be two concert violinists in town called William Brooke?'

Ellie's lips parted. 'You know him?'

'Yep. Known him for years. Not, I would have thought…' he looked her up and down '…essentially your type, Ellie.'

Ellie took a gulp of her wine this time. 'Before I get into what you perceive "my type" to be and how the hell you can know anyway—'

'He's gay.'

'*What?*'

Brett shrugged.

'But that's impossible!'

'You've turned him around?'

Ellie looked into those wry grey eyes and no amount of threatening to shoot herself stopped the tide of colour that rose to her cheeks. 'No! I mean I haven't even tried…I mean…I had no idea! Why would he want to take me to lunch and come to dinner—you must have it wrong!'

'Because he likes you, because he's interested in your kites—you could probably end up having a nice friendship with Will Brooke. If you were thinking of him in terms of a date, though...' He shrugged. 'That's a different matter.'

This time Ellie choked on her wine.

'I thought so,' Brett said.

'How would you know—anything?' she asked dangerously.

He gestured in the direction of the fridge. 'There is the matter of the new hairstyle, which is very attractive, incidentally. And according to Simon you don't usually paint your nails.'

Ellie drained her glass and handed it to him. 'I'll have another one, thank you.'

'Is that wise? So soon, I mean?'

'It's about the wisest thing I've done for years, Brett Spencer,' she told him. 'I have now added to the list of my dates—the list of a back-to-nature freak; an incredibly pretentious artist; an unbelievably pompous father-figure—a gay violinist! I can't believe it.'

He poured her another glass of wine. 'What about the one who tipped Simon five bucks to make himself scarce?'

She gazed at him over the rim of her glass. 'He was married. Of course I didn't know it until, well, I won't bore you with the details.'

'Ellie...' Brett started to laugh, and the phone rang.

She picked it up and said a few words into it, finishing off with, 'No, no, *please* don't worry! I haven't gone to any trouble at *all*!' And she put it down with a sigh of relief.

'Will can't make it?' Brett hazarded.

'Will can't make it,' she agreed. 'You have no idea

how embarrassed I feel—what a fool I could have made of myself!'

He grinned. 'You probably would have realized before it got to that stage—why did he put it off?'

'They've got a concert coming up in a couple of days and the conductor has called for an extra rehearsal this evening—I could kiss him!' She whirled around a couple of times and planted a kiss on the top of Simon's head as he came back into the kitchen.

Simon screwed up his face. 'What's with you now, Mum?'

'You're off the hook, kid. Mr Brooke can't make it tonight.'

'Brilliant!' Simon responded. 'So there's just the three of us!'

'Uh, well, I didn't mean that necessarily. He's still a nice person and I'd like to see him again but I won't be asking him to teach you the violin—' She stopped as the doorbell rang. 'Must be one of your mates, Simon. Ask him if he'd like to stay for dinner. We've got more than enough, now.'

But as Simon disappeared she said in a rapid undertone to Brett, 'We could have a problem, you know.'

'With Simon?'

'Yes! Didn't you hear what he said earlier?'

'I heard. Is it out of the question, Ellie?'

Her eyes widened and she suddenly had difficulty breathing. 'Are you suggesting…what I think you're suggesting?'

'I'm suggesting that you need a bit of help—' He stopped as Simon, close by, could be heard talking to his mate. 'Later,' he said.

But 'later' turned out to be nearly a week away because by the time Simon was in bed that evening Brett told her that he had a headache, probably only jet lag, but since he couldn't seem to think straight would she mind if they postponed their discussion?

Ellie agreed with alacrity and told him to go to bed.

The next morning, when he didn't appear after she'd got Simon off to school, she decided she'd better check on him.

His bedroom was in darkness and there was no movement. She was just about to close the door and let him sleep on when he groaned. She hesitated, then crossed the room to pull one curtain back. The sight that met her eyes as she turned back to the bed was far from reassuring.

The bed was a mess as if he'd been twisting and turning all night and he himself, as he sat up groggily, looked distinctly unwell. His eyes were heavy-lidded, he was hot and feverish and completely disorientated.

'Brett, what's wrong?' she asked. 'Surely this can't be jet lag?'

He stared at her, blinking dazedly until, she gathered, she fell into place, then he dropped his head into his hands with another heartfelt groan.

'I think we better get a doctor,' she said with some concern.

'I am a doctor.'

'Well, maybe, but—'

'Ellie, it's the flu, that's all.' He lay back and closed his eyes.

'How can you be so sure?' She crossed to the bed and looked down at him, noting the beading of sweat on his forehead.

'I've seen enough of malaria, yellow fever, sleeping sickness, cholera and the like in the past five years to know the difference. Besides which I spent a few days in Johannesburg with friends—one of them had it—it's rampant in Jo'burg at the moment.'

'Don't you think we ought to get—' she thought rapidly '—a blood test just to be on the safe side?'

He grimaced. 'All right, Florence Nightingale.'

'I'll be right back,' she retorted with a grin.

By the time the doctor arrived, she'd made Brett shower, she'd made up his bed freshly and she'd made him a hot lemon drink—he didn't want to eat anything.

The doctor was of the opinion that Brett was right, it was influenza, with the symptoms possibly accentuated by jet lag, but he also said it never hurt to err on the side of caution. He left after taking a blood sample and cautioning Ellie to allow him plenty of bed rest and plenty of fluids.

For the next couple of days Brett slept mostly, ate very little and put up with her ministrations, as in trying to keep him comfortable and peaceful without a murmur.

Then he sat up one morning when she brought his breakfast and swore comprehensively.

'I beg your pardon?' She paused beside the bed with the tray in her hands.

'Not you,' he said urgently. 'My bloody overnight bag! Has it turned up yet?'

Ellie put the tray across his knees, took her own cup of coffee from it and sat down in an armchair. 'No. Sorry, I forgot about it. Is—' she frowned '—it so important? Most people carry books, duty-free stuff and toiletries in their overnight bags.'

'Most people...' he eyed her sardonically in her fresh yellow cotton dress with little green sprigs on it '...carry stuff they don't want to be parted from in their overnight bags,' he disagreed.

'Such as?' She raised an eyebrow at him, then spied the one he'd brought home by mistake. It was standing at the bottom of the bed and she got up and opened it.

'I've been through it a dozen times; there's no clue to the owner's address,' he said impatiently.

She shrugged and began to pull stuff out of the bag item by item.

There was a book, two magazines, a toilet bag, a small stuffed dog—a child's toy or a mascot perhaps—some duty-free perfume and a camera. The toilet bag revealed cosmetics, very expensive ones.

'She was a woman—the person sitting next to you who might have picked up the wrong bag?'

'She was a woman,' he agreed sardonically.

Ellie pursed her lips, deducing that something about his fellow passenger had not endeared her to him. 'She doesn't seem to have anything she can't live without in this bag,' she commented.

'Well, I did! I had a very important research file and I also had the disk it was backed up onto.' He gazed at her broodingly.

Ellie fought her instincts for a long moment. Brett Spencer might be dynamite when he was fighting fit but over the last days she'd seen another side of him. A side that showed her he hated being sick and that he was restless even as ill as he felt. It had also brought her a lot closer to him physically than she'd ever been. And as she'd watched him try to be a good, grateful patient at the same time as she'd been exposed to him often only wearing short pyjama bottoms, she'd been both awed at how beautifully he was made and she was conscious of a growing affection.

In fact what she would like to do right now was slip

her arms round him and tell him not to worry, she would get his bag back come hell or high water...

She sat down again, picked up her cup and cleared her throat. 'OK, give me all the details and I'll ring them for you. Do you know her name?'

'Kylie Jones. But what I need is an address.' He looked down at the tray and realized for the first time that she'd cooked him a fragrant herb omelette and there was glass of freshly squeezed orange juice plus a pot of real coffee. And that for the first time in days, he felt hungry. He sighed. 'Look, I don't know how to thank you, Ellie, and I'm sorry if it sounded as if I was swearing at you.'

'Be my guest,' she murmured, hiding an inward tremor as he smiled—admittedly a low voltage one of the real thing—at her. 'I'll get on to them right away, but I also have to go to work this morning—will you be all right? I managed to rearrange my days for the last few days but—'

'I'll be fine, Ellie.' He reached for her hand. 'Thank you so much, you've been a brick.'

Oh, dear, Ellie thought as she got ready for work and remembered the feel of his hand over hers, much more of this and I'll be...what?

It wasn't until late that afternoon that she was able to report any progress to Brett.

She made them some tea and took it into him. 'You need the constitution of an ox to deal with this kind of thing,' she said ruefully. 'They keep putting you on hold and promising to call you back but, anyway, the gist of the matter is this. They cannot reveal names or addresses of passengers but they are doing their utmost to track down the person on the passenger list who was sitting

next to you. However, they're a bit baffled themselves
because no one else has come forward with a "wrong
bag" claim.'

She poured the tea and put his cup and a slice of cake
on the bedside table. 'How do you feel?'

'Health-wise or state-of-mind-wise?'

'I think I can gauge your state of mind.'

He looked faintly amused. 'Do I resemble a bear with
a sore head?'

'Uh—disgruntled, disillusioned, disenchanted and—'

'Disgustingly weak,' he supplied.

She sipped her tea. 'But better at all?'

He sat up and reached for his cake. 'Thanks to your
tender loving care, Ellie, yes, I'm starting to feel human
again.'

'Good. By the way, it is only the flu, the tests came
back this afternoon. And, on your behalf, I threatened
the airline that I would ring them hourly on the hour
until the matter was resolved.'

One dark eyebrow shot up. 'What did they say to
that?'

'I think they were tempted to offer me a free flight
out of the country!'

He laughed.

'Anyway, they're a lot less inclined to fob me off
with, "We have this matter in hand, Mrs Spencer"—
I—uh—told them I was your wife.'

He raised his eyebrows but said, 'You're a gem, Ellie.
How's Simon? I haven't heard much of him lately.'

'He's being very quiet so as not to disturb you. I
thought it was wise to keep him away for a while anyway.'

'I guess so. But he seems to have got over all his
childhood ailments.'

'Touch wood, he has.'

Brett drank his tea, then lay back with one arm behind his head and looked at her thoughtfully. She hadn't changed out of her trim uniform, a white blouse with navy trim and a short straight navy skirt. She wore stockings, navy shoes with little heels and her medical badge was pinned to her collar. She looked capable but chic.

'Is that where you acquired your nursing skills? From nursing Simon?'

She smiled. 'What skills? All I've done is make your bed and keep you supplied with clean pyjamas.'

'You've done a lot more than that. You've fed me, provided a peaceful environment, medicated me with…tisanes and hot lemon drinks and all the while you've been peaceful and restful about it.'

She thought for a bit. 'I suppose if I did pick up anything from Simon's early years it was that to be peaceful and restful helped.'

He moved. 'I should be up and about tomorrow.'

'I know this is a bit presumptuous since you're the doctor, Brett, but my advice is to take it easy.'

'I'm bored,' he said flatly.

'Well, that's a good sign, but all the same—if you feel like reading now, how about I bring you some books or—?'

'And lonely.'

Their gazes clashed. 'Ah. OK,' she said, thinking quickly. 'I'm working on a kite so once I've got dinner out of the way—Simon is spending the night with a friend—if you really feel like getting up for a bit, you could help or just sit and talk to me.'

'My pleasure, ma'am. What's for dinner?'

'Now that is a good sign,' she told him laughingly.

When she'd gone to deal with dinner, Brett found

himself contemplating several matters. Such as the fact that this might be his home, but nevertheless it now seemed very much Ellie's home. Her personality was imprinted on it, it ran smoothly thanks to her organisation and both house and garden seemed to have a bloom to them although she'd changed almost nothing.

The 'bloom' of a much-loved home? he wondered. If so, what did that say about Ellie the person, Ellie the woman, Ellie—who had been so wary of his plans for her life but had never moved on?

Dinner was simple, but it was artistically presented and delicious. Grilled Atlantic salmon, a potato focaccia and a rocket salad with black olives and shredded Spanish onions.

Afterwards he sat with her for a while in the enclosed back veranda where she had her design desk and all her kite-making equipment and discovered there was more to kite-making than he'd realized. And it came to him when she told him how much her kites sold for and how many repeat customers she had that the nest egg he'd treated so lightly might be much more substantial than he'd guessed.

He watched her as she expertly measured, sawed and bevelled dowling. She'd changed into her yellow cotton dress but wore a butcher's apron over it and had tied her hair back exposing an unexpectedly slender neck with damp curls clinging to it—it was a warm, humid night— and he asked her how she'd come to be such an expert.

She looked up with the little gold flecks in her eyes most noticeable. Then a shadow crossed those rather remarkable eyes. 'My father taught me. We used to fly our kites together.'

'Happy memories, Ellie?'

'I think I told you that my mother died when I was ten? Well, my stepmother and I…just didn't hit it off. It was only after Simon was born that I realized why she was so jealous even of little things like Dad and I making and flying kites. She couldn't have children of her own. The ultimate tie to him she craved, I guess.'

For a moment Ellie sat quite still staring down the years then she shrugged and her nimble fingers resumed work.

And Brett thought, So that explains it. That lack of confidence in Ellie Madigan, that tantalizing vulnerability about her he remembered rather suddenly…

'Tell me about your job?' he suggested, and was gratified to see her brighten.

In fact she became animated as she told him how she seemed to be having quite a bit of success with children who stuttered and they discussed it medically for a while.

Then he said, 'You obviously have a way with kids as well, Ellie.'

She glanced at him through her lashes. 'I would say you have too, Brett.'

He shrugged. 'What makes you say that?'

'Oh, the way Simon took to you virtually on sight. Considering the fact that he thought you were the new man in my life—' she grimaced '—that was quite a feat.'

He looked at her humorously. 'I've always found it especially either heart-wrenching or gratifying to work with children. So we have that in common,' he added almost to himself.

Ellie glinted him a questioning look.

He said nothing, however, and presently took himself to bed after thanking her for a nice evening. It shouldn't have surprised him but it did touch him to find that his bed had been remade and there was a flask of juice beside it.

Ellie made herself a cup of tea one evening and wandered out onto the terrace. Brett had been home for a week and was recovered from the worst of his virus so she was beginning to wonder what lay ahead.

But it had been a busy week and she laid her head back and could only think that October was a pretty month in Brisbane. The jacaranda at the bottom of the garden was in full bloom, the African tulip tree beside the drive was dropping its waxy scarlet blooms and the hibiscus hedge beside the pool was in full flower. Not that she could see the wonderful colours but the white, mauve and violet blooms of the several 'yesterday, today and tomorrow' bushes she'd planted beside the terrace were perfuming the night air.

Brett was on the phone once again exhorting the airline to track down his overnight bag.

She sat down in a basket chair, pushed off her shoes and studied the pool, a crystal blue with its underwater lighting. Presently, something alerted her to his presence. 'Pull up a chair,' she invited without turning her head 'Would you like a cup of tea?'

'No, thanks.' He sat down and clasped his hands between his knees.

Ellie tucked her feet up. 'Any luck?'

'No. The passenger in question is still not at home at the address they have listed. Thanks to you they're sending someone out on a daily basis, though.'

'Damn—I suppose there's not a lot more they can do.'

'No.' He studied his hands for a moment with an expression she couldn't identify, then he shrugged and looked directly into her eyes. 'So what do you think, Ellie?'

Ellie didn't pretend to misunderstand. 'About you and I—and the future? I don't know what you're proposing,' she said slowly.

'Maintaining the status quo for the time being.'

'Brett, that's fairly complicated—'

'I don't see why it should be.'

She glinted him an ironic little look. 'I have the strong feeling that my difficulties in getting Simon to relate to any men in my life will only increase once he has *you* in his life.' She gestured. 'On a full-time basis.'

He sat back and crossed his hands behind his head. 'That could have been a simple matter of the wrong choices, Ellie.'

She finished her tea and put her cup back carefully in the saucer. 'OK, my choices may not have been that inspired—'

'Have you ever fallen in love again—as opposed to wanting to enhance your son's life?'

She was silent.

'I guess it happened for you with Tom so you must have an idea of how it feels.'

She swallowed something in her throat. 'No, not like that. I don't think it can ever happen quite like that for me again.'

'Or it may—' he smiled at her '—suddenly spring up out of the sidewalk and hit you on the head.'

I wish you wouldn't smile at me like that, she thought crazily.

'Brett, there's one thing I don't understand—what's in it for you?' She saw him arrange his thoughts. He was sitting in a shaft of lamplight spilling out on to the terrace from the lounge.

He looked around. 'I'm at a bit of a loose end, to be honest.'

'You…regret coming back?'

He shrugged—with a trace of unease, she thought. 'No, but the transition from that kind of life to this—well, it's going to take some adjusting. So, what's in it for me at the moment? I feel at home here with you and Simon.'

Ellie felt a pleasant little glow and enjoyed the thought that she might be able to pay Brett back in this way. But presently she frowned. 'Brett, you've been a bit scathing about my love life, or lack of it,' she said dryly, 'but what about you? Before you took off for places like the Congo, you weren't exactly a loner.'

'Perhaps not,' he conceded, 'but marriage and what I've wanted to do with my life so far just haven't been compatible.'

'That would be true,' she agreed wryly. 'Although it doesn't rule out someone in the same line of work.'

He laid his head back. 'Perhaps we're both loners in a certain sense, Ellie. Me because of my work and you because of losing Tom.'

'What's that supposed to mean—?' She stopped as she heard footsteps coming up the drive and someone calling her name softly.

Brett lifted his head and frowned. 'Who…?'

'Dan Dawson,' she said. 'You remember the people who live next door? Dan is their son. He works on an oil rig and spends some of his time off with them. Hi, Dan!' She waved to the big young man crossing the lawn towards them. 'Do you remember Brett Spencer? He's come home.'

As it turned out, they remembered each other and, after shaking hands, Dan sat down with them. He was twenty-six and over the years he and Ellie had become friends. When he was home, he quite often called on her. He also appeared pleased to meet up with Brett again and brought him up to date on his career. At present he was stationed on an oil rig in the Timor Sea.

But when he got up to go, things took an unexpected turn. He said goodnight to Ellie but asked Brett if he could have a moment of his time. Brett looked surprised but suggested they step into the kitchen.

Ellie watched them go with a frown, then succumbed to her curiosity and crept round the terrace to a vantage point outside the kitchen window.

She arrived in time to hear Dan Dawson say to Brett Spencer, 'I've been keeping an eye on Ellie—when I'm home.'

'That's good of you, Dan,' Brett replied.

'As a matter of fact,' Dan continued, looking both embarrassed but determined, 'although I haven't told Ellie this yet, she's the one who keeps me sane sometimes. Oil rigs can be bloody boring, but I've got a picture of her next to my bunk. Just thought,' he said as Ellie's mouth dropped open, 'I'd let you know, old man. Because my contract is due to expire shortly and I'm thinking of coming back to Brissie full time and proposing to her. It's what she needs now Simon is growing up.'

Ellie shut her mouth with a click and scuttled back to her chair, missing Brett's response, but a moment later both men emerged and Dan walked away down the drive with a wave.

'I don't believe it!' Ellie said as soon as he was out of earshot.

Brett grimaced. 'I wondered if you'd be tempted to eavesdrop. Well? Why not? He's nice enough.'

'Brett, when I first moved in here Dan was still at school!'

'You weren't that long out of it yourself. He's only four years younger, he doesn't appear to have alienated Simon—'

'But he's never said a word to me, I had no idea! Oh,' she groaned, 'how do I get myself into these things?'

'At least this is a genuine guy who would appear to have fallen in love with you.'

'There is one disadvantage—I haven't fallen in love with him,' she pointed out. 'That is the accepted reason to marry someone, isn't it? A mutual falling in love?'

'Sure,' he agreed. 'But Dan is right about one thing. Simon is growing up and you need help. You must be aware of this yourself or why else would you be experimenting with—?'

'Don't say it,' she warned.

He grinned.

'What did you say to Dan?' She eyed him frowningly.

He considered. 'I told him I had the same aspirations and may the best man win.'

Ellie closed her eyes. 'I don't think I heard you right.'

Brett studied her as her eyes remained closed, with a mixture of amusement and something else. Something that caused him to wonder if this woman hadn't lain on the back roads of his mind for a long time in a way he'd failed to identify... Why else would he be issuing challenges to the likes of Dan Dawson? Why else had he come home to stay? Why had *she* stayed in his home for so long? A question he'd asked himself before.

Then her lashes shot up and her eyes were accusing. 'This is a game for you, Brett! I don't appreciate it!'

He debated with himself for a moment. Was this the

right time to tell her how his thoughts were running? Or was Tom still firmly entrenched in her heart?

'Uh,' he said as her gaze didn't waver, even got fiercer, 'there's a certain territorial aspect involved, I guess. It may have led me to responding in kind. Don't say it,' he added softly as her expression changed. 'Men!'

After a frozen moment an involuntary smile curved her lips. 'How right you are,' she agreed, but unheatedly. 'Getting back to you, though,' she said slowly, 'in five years or whenever this bit of research is over, will you go off again?'

'That remains to be seen.'

Ellie stared out over the lawn and couldn't for the life of her understand what prompted her to say it, but she did. 'You didn't think I was good enough for Tom, did you, Brett?'

'What gave you that idea?'

She twisted her hands. 'I just got this feeling you thought I was a passing romance, a case of Tom sowing his wild oats. And when you found out about Simon,' she said baldly, 'it was almost as if you'd been expecting me to get myself into that situation.'

'Ellie…' He paused and sighed. 'It wasn't that you weren't good enough for Tom. But it did cross my mind that you were rather naive and unsure of yourself in those days—and that you might have been looking for more than Tom had in mind.'

Ellie flinched. 'We'll never know, will we?'

'I didn't—I shouldn't have said that—'

'Don't worry, I sometimes wondered it myself. It still doesn't get us any further forward.' She sighed suddenly.

'Why don't we have a trial period?'

She looked at him helplessly.

He laughed softly. 'I'm not proposing a bed of nails. Only a trial period of going on as we have been.'

'Is this what you came home in mind with, Brett?'

He sobered rather abruptly. 'I didn't have any preconceived plans—how could I? I didn't know what the situation was. But now I've got to know Simon…' he paused '…and I've seen how things are, it seems like a good idea. It is,' he said slowly, 'the only thing I can do for Tom, now.'

She stared at him for a long, long moment.

'Ellie, no disrespect intended towards your handling of Simon thus far—I think you've done a marvellous job with him. But it's going to get harder.'

She put her feet down onto the cooling tiles. A breeze had risen and it was lifting Brett's dark hair. She shivered suddenly and stood up.

'I'll think about it.'

He got up and came to stand in front of her so they were only inches apart. And he watched her intently, her slim outline in the long indigo dress she was wearing again, her shuttered expression when normally she was like an open book, her new hairstyle—did she spend a lot of time fiddling with it? he wondered. It looked refreshingly natural to him…

'Have I offended you?' he asked quietly.

Yes! Of course she didn't say it, but something in her heart said it for her as that frisson tiptoed up and down her spine again and she came alive, not only to him, but alive in a way no man had made her feel since Tom; achingly, dangerously starved of love…

'No, Brett,' she said with an effort. 'I can never repay you for all you've done for us so perhaps I'm…to be honest, I feel as if I've already imposed on you far more than I ever should have. That's why I really need to think about this. Goodnight.'

She checked Simon on her way to bed.

As usual, he'd fallen asleep with his lamp on and the latest *Guinness World Records* open beside him. As usual, his clothes were scattered everywhere. She tidied up quietly, put a bookmark in the book and put it on his bedside table. Then she simply stared down at her son for a while with new eyes. Was it because she lived with him all the time that the resemblance to Tom didn't strike her so much these days? Was it so long ago now, anyway, that Tom had faded in her consciousness in more ways than one? Or was Simon simply his own person to her now?

But it was true that it was getting harder as a single mother with a growing son. Take the 'skateboard, roller blade' dilemma, she thought ruefully. Most of Simon's friends had one or the other, if not both, but she hadn't agreed to either because of the visions she'd had of broken limbs or broken heads, although her excuse to date had been the expense. But were her injury concerns legitimate?

Would a man have a better idea of a boy's limitations? Would a man be better at enforcing the skullcap rule against peer pressure? Was she heading towards being a clinging, fearful mother, in other words?

Perhaps most of all, though, how *was* she going to provide Simon with a suitable role model?

She stared down at her sleeping child, then switched the lamp off and left the room quietly.

Her bedroom was a lovely room, serene, spacious and furnished in buttery creams and jade green. On this night she prowled around restlessly, however, once she'd changed into her pyjamas, until she finally forced herself to sit down at the dressing table, and, in the process of applying cleansing cream to her face, come face to face with her other dilemma—Brett Spencer as a man.

And the shocking revelation that he *had* offended her this evening because his proposition—even though she'd made him feel at home—was mostly based on helping with Simon. Which meant…?

When did it happen? she asked herself helplessly as she tissued off the cleansing cream and reached for her toner. Of course, he'd always been attractive, but it was one thing to acknowledge that in a man and another to feel desolated, as she did now, about him having no interest in her as a woman.

It was quite another matter to ponder whether, of all the batterings life had handed out to her, this might be the worst. And just when she'd thought she was doing so well, apart from the problem of a role model for Simon.

Then she stared at herself in the mirror and was forced to acknowledge it couldn't have happened in the space of one week. So, for how long had she been burying in her subconscious the fact that she'd fallen in love with Brett Spencer? Way back to when he'd rescued her from public humiliation beside a parking meter?

She took an appalled breath. Was that why she'd always refused to admit it? Was that why she could never admit it to anyone but herself without being unfaithful to the memory of Tom?

If only he hadn't come home, she thought despairingly. If only she'd got herself out of this position years ago. And how to deal with living under the same roof indefinitely? It might have been eleven years ago, but she could still vividly recall that fighting Brett when he'd made up his mind was not something she had excelled at previously.

You were also battling nausea, panic, grief and loneliness at the time and then the threat of pre-eclampsia, she pointed out to herself.

She patted toner onto her face and finally took herself to bed. But her dilemma didn't leave her, in fact it got worse as she contemplated one scenario after another. Brett having mistresses, for example, while he pursued the jolly cause of providing Simon with a role model. Had he kept up his apartment? she wondered. Because he wouldn't be able to bring them to 3 Summerhill Crescent, Balmoral.

And what would he expect of her in that line, not being privy to the fact that no other man would do for her now—not ever being privy to that fact if she could help it? Perhaps—that they could roster his apartment, she thought rather grimly.

Oh, no, was her final thought before she fell asleep; it simply couldn't work!

She was slow and dithery the next morning, and only just got Simon off in time for school. Fortunately it wasn't a work day for her, and Brett wasn't up yet.

So she brewed a pot of coffee and had a leisurely cup to get herself into a better gear and was about to start the housework when the front door bell rang.

She froze for a moment, thinking of Dan Dawson— yet another complication in her messy life!—but relaxed as she remembered that Dan always used the kitchen door. She was quite unprepared, however, for the girl who stood on the other side of the front door with an overnight bag in her hand. A stunning, extremely shapely blonde with true violet eyes, poured into a cyclamen stretch top and black leather trousers.

'Hello?' Ellie said. 'Can I help you?'

'I hope so,' the blonde replied, and put the bag down. 'Does Brett Spencer live here?'

Enlightenment hit Ellie—the bag was identical to the one in Brett's bedroom. 'You must be from the airline! Look, he'll be so glad to get his bag back.' She put the bundle of washing she had in her arms down on the hall bench and opened the screen door.

'I'm not from the airline,' the other girl said wryly. 'I'm his fellow passenger—we had a great flight together!—and I must have picked up the wrong bag by mistake and I carted it all the way to Melbourne. Lucky there was an address inside his bag because there isn't one in mine. But I'd really like to hand it over personally, not only because I feel such a clot, but because I want to explain that I got the flu, that's why it's taken me so long to bring it back.'

'You—so you must be Kylie Jones?'

'He told you about me? Great! Because I've got a thing or two to prove to Brett Spencer.'

'Such as?' Ellie enquired dazedly.

'Between you, me and the gatepost—' the girl lowered her voice conspiratorially '—he may not think I'm the right girl for him, but I've decided to prove him wrong. By the way, my name is Chantal, I don't use Kylie any more.' She smiled at Ellie in a friendly way. 'I guess you must be the cleaning lady?'

Ellie's mouth dropped open as her brain synapses fizzed and spun beneath the weight of all this information. Then she looked down at herself. Her jeans were old and frayed. Her T-shirt, once bright pink, was now faded and had tangled with a non-colourfast navy-blue item in a long-ago wash. Her sandals were very comfortable but of a vintage that prohibited her from wearing them in public...

'You could say that,' she conceded at last. 'I certainly do a lot of cleaning. But he's not up yet so—'

'Yes, I am. Chantal, you didn't have to do this.'

Ellie swung round. Brett was standing behind her, obviously not long out of bed. His hair was hanging in his eyes, his shirt was hanging out of his cargo pants and his feet were bare. He looked moody and singularly unimpressed with this turn of events, but sensationally sexy at the same time.

And as if she, Ellie, did not exist, Chantal said with a secret, sexy little smile of her own, 'Oh, yes, I did, Brett. Why don't you ask me in for a cup of coffee? I've come a long way to restore your bag to you and I would have done it a lot sooner but I got the flu and went to stay with my mum for some TLC.'

Afterwards, Ellie was never sure why she acted as she did. At the time, she acted on impulse and—instinct? Whatever, she immediately invited Chantal in, adding, 'There's a pot of coffee on the stove, as it happens!' And she resolutely ignored Brett's steely gaze as she ushered Chantal in all her glory towards the lounge.

Brett followed, having retrieved his bag, which he put on a table and opened. And she thought she detected a genuine sigh of relief as he took out an envelope folder and a floppy disk container.

But just as Ellie was about to say she would have the coffee ready in two shakes of a duck's tail, he sent her another steely glance, then transferred his attention to Chantal. 'This is Ellie, Chantal. She's not the cleaning lady, we're living together.'

Oh, no, you don't, Brett Spencer! It shot through

Ellie's mind. Whatever is going on between you and this girl, you're not going to use me to get yourself out of it! No way!

'Not really living together, just sharing the same house at the moment, Chantal,' she said soothingly to the bitter look growing in those violet eyes. 'Why don't you explain it properly, Brett, while I get the coffee?'

'No, Ellie, sit down,' he ordered. 'You too, Chantal.' There was something so determined in his eyes, they both sank into chairs.

'Chantal,' he continued less severely, 'would I be right in assuming you deliberately switched overnight bags?'

Chantal looked momentarily discomforted.

'Since it was the only way you could come up with of staying in touch?' he continued rather gently.

This time Chantal shrugged with her lips twisting. 'Pretty clever, don't you think? Of course I had no way of knowing there would be an address in the bag but at least I had something to go to the airline with.'

By this time Ellie's synapses were short circuiting. 'Did you really switch bags?' she asked Chantal, her eyes almost standing out on stalks.

'Honey,' Chantal said, then grinned charmingly, 'if all you can get out of this guy is the sharing of a house, you might need to be a little inventive yourself!'

She stood up and smoothed her leather trousers. Then her gaze locked with Brett's. 'I decided to take your advice about not making certain assumptions at face value,' she said simply. 'I'm taking the Gold Coast job, I've got a flat in Brisbane and I'd really like to get to know you better. That's all. Bye for now—I'll let myself out!' And she left. Reminding Ellie, although their figures couldn't be more different, of the way Dan Dawson had sauntered down the drive last night although there was another, more subtle difference. There had been a slightly self-conscious aura to Dan last night whereas Chantal was not in the least self-conscious, she was just—superb. And Brett's gaze, although hard, stayed on the doorway for a long moment.

'All right,' Ellie said a few minutes later over a belated cup of coffee, 'I accept that you didn't intend to continue whatever it was you started with Chantal Jones on that long, boring flight. Mind you, I also take issue with that—you obviously got her hopes up in *some* way.'

Brett was silent but a faint grin tugged at his lips.

'And I take issue with the fact that you show not one ounce of remorse!'

'Ellie, all I did was talk to her. Then, when she made a rather obvious suggestion, I gave her some very good advice.'

'So I noticed—she's obviously taken it to heart, in fact!'

He shrugged.

And Ellie started to laugh softly. 'A topless dancer!'

He raised an eyebrow at her. 'She's actually quite a nice girl.'

Ellie sat up and sipped her coffee, still chuckling. 'She may be but I certainly don't feel such a dumb klutz about the errors of judgement I may have made in the past!'

'Well, I'm glad about that but I should point out that I have yet to make an error of judgement.'

'I'd like to bet my bottom dollar it was touch and go, Brett!' She looked across at him with her eyes sparkling with amusement.

He studied his cup and grimaced.

'Actually, I quite liked her.' Ellie looked wry. 'I

thought she handled herself with aplomb in the circumstances.'

'If you can handle yourself topless you can probably handle anything with aplomb.'

'What are you going to do about her?' Ellie asked.

'Nothing. What are you going to do about Dan Dawson?'

She frowned. 'Are you implying there is any similarity between the two cases? I never led Dan on in any way!'

'He does have a picture of you beside his bunk, Ellie.'

Words failed her briefly and when she could come up with anything, it sounded lame to her own ears. 'It's still not the same thing, I had no idea.'

'You're very judgemental for someone who wasn't even there,' he commented.

Ellie muttered something beneath her breath and stood up impatiently. 'Since I've been mistaken for the cleaning lady, I may as well get on with it!''

He grinned fleetingly. 'Chantal might have that effect on ninety per cent of the female population. I wouldn't take it to heart. And I need to take myself to work.' He paused, then touched her lightly on the chin with his knuckles. 'Why don't you give the cleaning a miss for a change? The place looks fine to me.'

How like a man, Ellie thought darkly as she methodically got through her chores, and could not, for the life of her, imagine Chantal washing floors. And later in the day, her woes were compounded when Dan Dawson came to call.

She found him hovering in the kitchen doorway looking embarrassed.

'Oh—hi, Dan!'

'Ellie, can I come in?'

'Sure,' she said and hoped the sense of helplessness she felt didn't come across in her voice. 'Sit down, if you like.'

But Dan told her that he preferred to stand and immediately embarked on a long and tangled explanation that nevertheless contained the kernel of what he'd told Brett the previous evening.

Nor was Ellie able to get a word in edgeways until he finished his monologue with the observation that at least it was out in the open now.

Ellie sank into a chair and wished herself at the South Pole. It didn't happen, of course, and there was no dodging the hopeful look in Dan's blue eyes.

She swallowed. 'Dan, I can't tell you how flattering this all is,' she began. 'But…I think I'm too old for you—'

'No way, Ellie! Anyway, I prefer older women,' he replied fervently.

'But I had no idea!'

'That's because I'd rather be subtle about these things,' he said proudly. 'People look at me and don't think I could have a subtle bone in my body—you know, oil-well rigger, tough and all that—but that's not the real me.'

Ellie stared at him. He was no taller than Brett but a lot broader and all of it hard muscle. He had the neck and shoulders of a front-row forward, very large hands and feet, but he wasn't bad-looking with thick fair hair and rather shy blue eyes. As a friend, he'd been fun, but what to do now?

'Dan, I never thought you were unsubtle. In fact it's been a real pleasure to know you but I just don't think of you in the same way.'

'Is it because of Brett?'

'No! Good heavens, no!' It was out before she could help herself and not only was it a lie but a tactical error because Dan relaxed visibly.

'Maybe you just need a bit of time to get used to the idea?' he suggested. 'Why don't you think about it?'

'No, thank you, Dan,' she said firmly. 'And you definitely must not give up your job because of me—'

'Don't worry about that,' he interposed with a grin. 'I've had my fill of oil rigs, I've saved a small fortune and I'm ready to lead a normal life now. You and Simon wouldn't want for anything,' he confided. 'So have a think, Ellie.'

His gaze rested on her with an awful mixture of pride and tenderness—awful, because she couldn't reciprocate and she hated to hurt his feelings—and Simon came pelting through the back door.

'Hey, dude!' he said to Dan. 'I didn't know you were home! Would you like to have a go at the new video game my grandad sent me?'

CHAPTER FOUR

'YOU'RE looking very pensive, Ellie. Anything wrong?'

It was the same day but late in the evening. Brett had stayed out for dinner and just come home to find Ellie curled up in the lounge staring into space.

She stirred. 'My life has just spun completely out of control, if you really want to know.'

He grinned. 'Tell me?'

She hesitated, then shrugged. 'I've had an offer of marriage.'

'Dan came over to state his case?' he hazarded.

'He did.'

'And you were able to let him down nicely?'

Ellie gazed at him broodingly. He wore jeans and a black polo shirt and was looking lean and strong from his broad shoulders down to his thick-soled black shoes. Not only lean and strong but terrifyingly attractive.

She released a slow breath. 'It was like knocking my head against a brick wall.'

Brett sat down on a chintzy settee opposite her and rested his chin on his hand with a grimace. 'How did you go about it?'

'I tried to tell him I was too old for him.'

'A bit of a cop out,' he suggested wryly. 'What did he say to that?'

'He *prefers* older women.'

'Ellie,' Brett said, when he stopped laughing, 'why didn't you just tell him the truth?'

'I did!' She looked tragic. 'But he insisted I think

about it. It was all so—I mean, I didn't want to hurt his pride and—the sum total, I guess, is that this has to have been just about the most unromantic day of my life and there have been a few of those.'

Brett sobered. 'You know,' he said slowly, 'the kindest thing to do is simply to say no, thanks, Dan—rather than letting it drag on and keeping his hopes alive.'

'I did that as well,' she said. 'It just bounced off him. Incidentally, is that how you handled Chantal Jones?'

His lips twitched. 'Point taken, Ellie. But I did in fact tell her—quite pointedly—that I was not the man for her.'

'What say Dan is as stubborn as Ms Jones?'

'Just stick to your line. At least he has an oil rig he has to go back to shortly.'

Ellie sighed. 'I think I'll go to bed.'

'No, stay a while.' He got up and disappeared into the kitchen and came back with a glass of wine for her and a brandy for himself.

And he waited until she'd sipped some of her wine before he said, 'Is the lack of romance in your life getting to be a problem, Ellie?'

She nearly choked on a sip of wine and the look she flashed him was full of hurt before she could compose herself.

'I meant—' she stood up resolutely and said with dignity '—that on top of being mistaken for the cleaning lady by Chantal Jones, being told by a man who then went off to play video games with my son that Simon and I would want for nothing if I married him...was all a bit lowering.'

'I see what you mean,' Brett replied gravely and stood up himself. 'Well, then, would this help?' His gaze wandered up and down her white cotton blouse tucked into colourful, flower-printed shorts. 'While you were being such a cool, calm and efficient nurse there were times when I—barely—restrained myself from pulling you into bed with me and rendering you a lot less cool and calm.'

Ellie's lips parted incredulously.

'Don't look so surprised. You were also very sweet and there is—' he put his hands around her waist, nearly spanning it '—an awful lot of sweetness packed into this slender frame.' His gaze dwelt on her breasts. 'I cannot,' he went on simply, 'get it out of my mind.'

Ellie tried to speak but nothing came out.

'Then there's your perfume.'

'I don't wear perfume, it makes me sneeze,' she did manage to say at last.

He smiled slightly. 'That's what's so nice about it. Clean and fresh and—just you. And the way your hair curls.'

He paused and she felt his breath fan her forehead, then he went on. 'So, you see, Ellie, on this day in fact, you have two men very much taken with you. I would call that *quite* romantic.'

'Brett, if this is designed to massage my ego,' she breathed, stunned, 'you—'

'Not at all,' he denied as he slid his hands up beneath her breasts and watched intently for her reaction.

Ellie trembled and did battle with the mental images that came to her—of being pulled into his bed and made love to. But there was so much else to battle, how his hands below her breasts were causing her nipples to tingle, a sure sign they were about to misbehave themselves. How his proximity and that intent query in his grey eyes were weakening factors, as if her body had a mind of its own and was hell-bent on melting with desire beneath Brett Spencer who was tall and strong and everything she wanted.

She swallowed and told herself to resist this, but he was more than a match for her. He touched each burgeoning nipple beneath her cotton shirt with his thumbs and a streak of pure, hot sensuality flowed through her, causing her to gasp again although this time with delight.

'Ellie?' he said then, very softly, and pulled her close so he could kiss her and at the same time demonstrate that he was by no means unaffected.

When they separated finally, her heart was beating like a runaway train, she was gloriously alive to the splendours of Brett Spencer and the way he made her feel in his arms. As if she couldn't get enough of him, and the finesse he employed. His touch on her most sensitive spots and the little questions he sometimes asked with his eyes—Is this OK?—and the way her body answered for her—Yes, oh, yes! The way he kissed not only her mouth but the soft hollows at the base of her throat, and the way he showed her that he was quite capable of driving her crazy with desire...

It was Simon who saved her, although it took her a little while to admit that she needed or wanted to be saved. But no sooner had they parted to catch their breath than they heard his door open and her maternal instincts took over in a flash, so that by the time Simon found them in the lounge she was back sitting in her chair trying to look as normal as possible.

'What's doing, guys?' Simon enquired as he rubbed his eyes like a sleepy owl. His hair was standing up at the crown and his pyjama jacket was buttoned up crookedly.

'Nothing much,' Brett said from his position at the

bay window where he'd been looking out over the darkened garden. 'Can't you sleep?'

Simon pulled a face. 'I was dreaming of skateboards—Mum, if I do the chores I do for pocket money for free for a while, would you be able to afford one then?'

Ellie opened her mouth but Brett spoke first. 'I think it would be a better idea if you saved your pocket money so you could buy yourself one.'

'That could take years!' Simon objected. 'I'd be old and grey by the time I could afford it.'

'I doubt it.' Brett looked amused. 'And there is one way you could augment your earnings. You could clean my car once a week.'

Simon hesitated. 'Would you also teach me to drive it?'

'No!' Ellie spoke at last.

'Your mum's right, you're too young for that, mate.'

'Thank you,' Ellie said with a trace of bitterness.

Simon eyed her, then turned his attention back to Brett. 'How much?'

Brett named a sum and Simon did some mental calculations that appeared to satisfy him to an extent. He said with a shrug, 'It's still going to take a while, but not as long as what Mum had in mind, I guess. Unless you'd like to loan me the money?' he suggested to Brett. 'I could pay you back interest.'

'Simon!' Ellie expostulated.

But Brett said, 'No, old man. First principle of sound economic management—don't get yourself into hock if you can avoid it.'

Simon considered, then shrugged. 'OK. At least I might be able to sleep now.' And he took himself back to bed.

Ellie waited until she heard his door close, then she said to Brett, 'How dare you? I'm not sure I want him to have a skateboard in the first place!'

Brett came over to sit down opposite her again. 'Ellie,' he said quietly, 'he's a boy. You can't coddle him.'

'There's a difference between coddling and wanting to protect him from all sorts of horrific injuries.'

'He rides his bike around the place, doesn't he?'

'Yes, but the streets are very quiet round here—' She broke off and sighed suddenly. 'I know what you're saying and I don't *want* to be become a fearful mother, but it's not easy.'

He said nothing, but just stared at her thoughtfully until she began to feel all hot and bothered at the memory of what had taken place before Simon had intervened.

'Ellie?'

She stirred and smoothed her shorts. 'I don't know what got into me. Could we just forget about it, please?'

He said one word. 'How?'

Her gaze flew to his, then skittered away as she detected a momentary glint of compassion in his eyes, which was the last thing she wanted from Brett Sponoor, she now knew.

'Has there been *anyone* serious in your life since Tom?' he asked then.

She looked away, but there didn't seem to be any point in dissembling. 'No.'

'No one who made you feel the way I—*we* did—not so long ago?' he persisted.

A tinge of colour stole into her cheeks but she said straightly, 'No. And that's another reason not to place too much...' She paused, searching for the right word.

'Credence on it?' he suggested, but rather dryly.

'Brett—' she held his gaze deliberately '—this is not that easy to admit but it occurred to me a few days ago that I was thirty and essentially dateless and desperate. Well, not *desperate*, but, yes, starting to realize that…life was passing me by.'

'So you're saying any reasonable man could have produced that effect in you, Ellie?'

She bit her lip and wondered why he wasn't a lawyer instead of a doctor. Then she decided to be a bit lawyerly herself. 'Perhaps any reasonable woman could have produced that effect in you, Brett? If you're on the rebound from Africa, a bit unsettled and at a loose end?'

'On the other hand, and I must stress that *you* brought this up,' he drawled, 'it could be said that I've knocked back Chantal Jones in favour of you, Ellie.'

Her lips parted and a little glint of indignation lit her eyes. 'Let's get this straight—you knocked back Ms Jones because she's a topless dancer!'

'On the contrary.' His lips twisted. 'That's a powerful inducement for a man. She's an awful lot of woman and very—willing.'

'I…I don't see the connection!' she protested.

He stood up and looked down at her with definite irony in his eyes. 'I was just trying to point out the distinction between us. You appear to feel you're ripe for the taking and you appear to be accusing me of taking advantage of that. But there has to be more to it than that otherwise…well, that was why I mentioned Ms Jones.'

Ellie stood up and drew herself to her full height of five feet four. 'That is the worst case of twisted logic I've ever encountered!'

'Not really, if you think about it,' he murmured. 'Which I'll leave you to do now, Ellie. Goodnight.'

'Before you go, Brett, if anyone else tells me to "think" about something—I'll scream!'

'You really do need some romance in your life, Ellie,' he observed, and walked out.

Of course there was no way to stop herself from thinking about it.

In fact the only thing that was fortuitous about the next few days was the lack of Brett around the house to constantly remind her of what had happened. He became heavily involved in his grant and the setting up of his laboratory.

She also had to work three days in a row after that extraordinary encounter and get Simon away on a five-day school camp as well. He'd never been away from her that long before and she waved him off with a little pang; she'd also stayed up late the night before baking all sorts of goodies for him to take along.

In his absence she took the opportunity to put in more hours at work than she usually did. Not only, she freely acknowledged, in the cause of bettering her finances but because she was as confused as ever on the subject of Brett, and the less she saw of him, the better. She had already been to Dan's and dispensed with one of her worries. He'd been understandably hurt, but he'd accepted her refusal with a mixture of resignation and grace. They'd both agreed to remain friends.

But she still went hot and cold at the memory of being in Brett's arms and the circles of her mind on the subject of how they'd affected each other remained just that—circles. Curiously, however, it became a sore point with her that when they did happen to meet he made no reference to anything personal.

Or, she amended her thoughts, was the real problem that he didn't have to? Just to know he was in the house made her jumpy and skittish, she acknowledged with gloom, because 'skittish' was not how she liked to think of herself. Just to have him come to her aid when a prototype kite she was testing got stuck in a tree was a severe trial for her, for example.

The ladder was too short for her to reach the first branch and she was standing on the lawn looking frustrated when he came home. In five minutes he restored the kite to her, but watching him climb up and down the tree with fluid strength and ease awoke very similar sensations in her as he'd aroused a few nights previously. Causing her to be disjointed in her thanks, stilted, embarrassed and feeling like a girl suddenly aware of her sensuality for the first time.

If he noticed, he made no comment.

But on the Friday evening, before Brett got home, Chantal arrived for an unannounced visit.

She came bearing a cold magnum of French champagne and a gorgeous Barberton daisy in a pot for Ellie. Ellie explained that Brett wasn't home but Chantal shrugged and suggested they sample the champagne themselves.

It was a beautiful evening, it was the end of a particularly hard week, and Ellie found herself agreeing. So she got out some home-made cheese straws and they sat outside on the terrace.

'I guess Brett's told you all about me, the topless dancer et cetera, et cetera?' Chantal said.

'Well, yes, a bit.'

'And you don't take instant exception as in wanting to call me a whore and all the rest of it?'

Ellie grinned. 'Don't be silly! You're very welcome here.'

'How's he doing?'

'Brett? Uh…fine, as far as I can tell.'

'Any women friends lurking around the ridges?' Chantal enquired.

'No-o. Not so far.' *Help!* Ellie thought.

'Of course, it's only a matter of time. Guys like that don't grow on trees,' Chantal observed wisely.

'No, I guess not. How's the revue going?'

Chantal tipped a hand. 'OK. Not as lavish as Sun City but I'm enjoying it.'

'Thanks so much for the daisy!' The colourful flower in its pot was sitting on the terrace table next to the silver wine cooler.

'So tell me about yourself, Ellie, and how you come to be sharing a house with Brett?' Chantal invited.

'Oh, it's a long story.' But possibly better than discussing Brett, it shot through her mind. 'Briefly, though, it happened like this.'

At the end of it, Chantal raised her glass to Ellie. 'I'm impressed with how you've handled your life. Where's your kid?'

Ellie told her.

Chantal became thoughtful, then she said abruptly, 'Do you think I've got any chance with him, Ellie?'

'Chantal—' Ellie reached for the champagne and topped up their glasses '—to be honest, I have no idea. Oh!' She squinted down the driveway and saw Dan Dawson approaching.

'What?'

'Um…this man proposed to me recently. This could be a bit awkward,' Ellie replied helplessly.

'Tell you what, we could do each other a little favour here,' Chantal murmured as Dan drew nearer. 'If you were to ask me to stay on for dinner in the hope that Brett comes home and finds me here all legit, I could take care of it for you.'

'You could?' Ellie said blankly.

Chantal winked. 'It's all in a day's work, honey.'

Half an hour later Brett Spencer arrived home to find a jolly threesome on the terrace drinking champagne.

'Oh, there you are!' Ellie greeted him. 'Just in time, I was about to start dinner. Do sit down and entertain the guests while I tinker in the kitchen for a bit.' She got up and went indoors.

'Chantal. Dan,' Brett greeted them noncommittally. 'Excuse me for a moment, I need to—wash my hands.' And he disappeared indoors hot on Ellie's heels.

'What the hell's going on?' he enquired, cornering her in the kitchen.

'They both came to visit so I invited them to dinner,' Ellie said innocently.

'Are you mad—or drunk?' He looked her up and down, taking in her hot-pink bike shorts and sherbet-yellow stretch top.

She responded with an assessing gaze up and down his attire of moleskins, a check shirt and desert boots and replied with the golden glints in her eyes laughing at him, 'Neither. Well, I don't think it would be wise to have any more champagne, but I'm quite sane. Chantal is taking Dan's mind off things for me.' She tilted her chin at him.

'What do you mean?'

'If you go out there you'll probably see for yourself—it's really quite amusing. But I guess men will be men.'

'Ellie,' he said dangerously.

'Look, Brett,' she returned, suddenly feeling stone-cold sober, 'don't start lecturing me or laying down the law, I'm not in the mood—she's your problem, not mine. It so happens I quite like her.'

'What about Dan?'

'Dan…is no longer a problem. Now will you go outside while I get dinner? Otherwise I'm liable to do something I might regret.'

'Is this all because of what happened the other night?'

'Oh, that?' She shook her head. 'But I am missing Simon, I'm tired, overworked at the moment and it didn't seem like a bad idea to sit down and have a glass of champers.' She gestured with both hands palm out. 'Things just got complicated from there on.'

'Or three or four glasses?' he suggested.

'If I want to have six or eight, I will!'

'OK.' A reluctant smile twisted his lips. 'Calm down. I'll go and hold the fort.'

Fortunately, she had a frozen dish of stir-fry beef and rice, which she only had to heat and make a salad to go with it. And she set the table in the dining room, lit candles and called the faithful to dinner.

What conversation had taken place while she'd been in the kitchen, she had no idea, nor did she care.

As they sat down to eat, however, it was Chantal's chair that Dan pulled out. And it soon became apparent that he still couldn't take his eyes off her—not so surprising really, Ellie thought. Chantal in a Lurex boob tube with skin-tight leopard-skin print trousers and very high gold sandals was enough to poleaxe most men. And she'd hardly had to lift a finger to get Dan in.

Whether Brett was poleaxed, however, was impossible to tell, as was what he made of the situation, although he did play the good host. And Chantal continued to be mesmerizing, funny, gorgeous and she even helped clear up after the meal.

All the same, Ellie felt like Alice at the Mad Hatter's Tea Party when Chantal and Dan left together, at Brett's suave suggestion that Dan could see her to her car. And she collapsed into her chair and started to laugh until she got hiccups, although she hadn't missed the searching, lingering glance Chantal bestowed on Brett and the way he'd countered it—with a severely unreadable one of his own.

'Here.' Brett handed her a glass of brandy. 'It was all your idea.'

Ellie wiped her eyes. 'Talk about being let off the hook in the most demoralizing way possible!'

He sat down with his own brandy. 'You might have a better understanding now of the powers and perils of Ms Jones, Ellie. But I agree, it's a relief to be let off the hook.'

'Oh, I don't think you're off the hook, Brett!'

'If you didn't keep inviting her in and fostering a "women of the world unite against men!" spirit, I'd already be off the hook,' he said with some asperity.

Ellie subsided. 'Would she be out of the question if she wasn't a topless dancer?'

'No, it wouldn't be out of the question even as a topless dancer, she could well have a heart of gold. The thing is, though, you would probably resent it if I tried to matchmake for you?' He looked at her with considerable irony.

Ellie grimaced. 'Point taken.'

'Why have you stayed here for so long, Ellie?'

Her lips parted on the unexpected question and a glint of anxiety came to her eyes. 'You sound as if you don't approve—I'm sorry, you have every right not to...'

'It's not that at all. But you weren't very much in favour of the idea at the time and I guess I have to wonder why you haven't moved on in all these years.'

She swallowed and looked around. 'I...it became like an anchor for me, I suppose,' she said, 'although I have wondered if it wasn't the line of least resistance. But I seemed to feel safe here, then I grew to love it and I got involved in the garden.' She shrugged. And sighed. 'Nor can I ever thank you enough,' she added awkwardly, 'although I'm still determined to pay you my kite money.'

He sat down at the head of the table. 'I don't want payment, Ellie. And I sometimes think *I* took the line of least resistance. So far as helping with Simon.'

'Oh, no,' she assured him. 'Without what you did for me, our lives would have been so much more difficult.'

'In pecuniary terms, perhaps. There's a lot more to life than that, though.'

She said slowly, 'It's not your burden, Brett.'

He didn't answer, he seemed to be far away in fact, then, 'About what happened the other night.'

But Ellie stiffened immediately. 'I'd rather we forgot about that,' she said in a cool little voice.

'Why?'

'In case you're tempted to massage my ego once again.'

'I wasn't—'

'Oh, yes, you were,' she contradicted and shook her curls at him. 'Maybe you've forgotten; if so, let me re-

fresh your memory. Like today, I'd gone through two
rather demoralizing sessions, one with Chantal Jones and
one with Dan Dawson. The difference is that today I'm
not feeling sorry for myself at all!'

'Is that brandy on top of champagne talking?' he queried with a smile at the back of his eyes.

'Not at all,' she denied. 'It's pure Ellie Madigan who
doesn't like being patronized, Brett Spencer.'

He raised his eyebrows. 'Is that what you call it? I
would have said it fell into the category of a mutual...conniption, which, incidentally, I enjoyed very
much.'

She stared at him with pinched nostrils, then retreated
to her bedroom with her brandy barely tasted.

She got a phone call from Simon early the next morning.
There was a public phone at the camp that the kids were
encouraged to use if they felt homesick—not that it was
a problem for Simon.

'How's it going, Mum?' he said cheerfully down the
line. 'Not suffering any withdrawal symptoms?'

'I don't get your drift, dude,' she replied.

'Just thought you might be missing your only son.
I've never been away for so long before.'

'Oh. Ah. Well, I'm missing you madly, of course, but
I haven't gone into a decline yet. How's it going with
you?'

'Super,' he said enthusiastically. 'And on account of
all the things you baked for me to bring with me, I'm
just about the most popular boy in the camp. I tell you,
no kid could have a better mum.'

'That's very sweet of you, Simon,' she said a little
huskily.

'Now don't go all gooey,' he warned.

'Wouldn't *dream* of it!'

'How's it going with Brett?'

'Uh...fine! But...' she hesitated and frowned '...why do you ask?'

'Why don't you want him to know you like him a lot, Mum?'

The question down the line took her breath away. 'Simon, I don't...know what you mean.'

'Well, I just reasoned that if you don't mind him kissing you—'

'Simon!'

'OK, I wasn't spying on you. I had no idea what was going on when I came out that night so I turned round and went back, then I came in again and made more noise about it. It wasn't hard to see you were kinda shook up, Mum.'

Ellie was speechless.

'But, look, it's fine with me,' Simon went on. 'I think it's the best thing that could happen to you. He's real cool—hey, Mum, my money's running out, see you s—' The connection was cut by a series of beeps.

Ellie put the phone down slowly and went to make breakfast.

Brett was already at the kitchen table reading the paper. 'Morning,' he said. 'Who was that?'

She eyed him moodily. Now that he'd recovered, he always got up at the crack of dawn and went for a jog then a brisk swim in the pool and, for some reason, it annoyed her immensely to see him looking so fit and relaxed, big, vital, tousled, blue around the jaw and almost insanely attractive.

'That was my only son.' She got out a pan and some bacon and eggs.

He raised an eyebrow. 'Homesick?'

Ellie put the bacon on, then she removed a segment of mouth-wateringly ripe pawpaw from the fridge, scooped out the seeds and cut it into two segments. She squeezed fresh orange juice over them, a dash of sugar and topped each segment with fresh strawberries. 'On the contrary, he's having a ball.' She placed Brett's fruit in front of him.

'I see.' Brett looked down at the plate, then up into her eyes. 'Thanks. Ellie?'

But she turned away and went over to the stove where she busied herself with the bacon and eggs.

'All right,' she heard him say, 'how about lunch, then?'

'I've only just started breakfast,' she responded tartly. 'Isn't it a bit soon to be wanting lunch?'

'I was suggesting that I take you *out* to lunch.'

'What for?' She turned from the stove with a frown.

'It's Saturday, it's a lovely day and it may just take your mind off your only son, who is not missing you at all by the sound of it. Not that there's anything wrong with that,' he added, his grey eyes dancing. 'It only points to a well-adjusted kid. You could be a different matter, however.'

Ellie had a spatula in her hand, which she held aloft in outraged amazement. 'Are you saying *I'm* badly adjusted?'

He grimaced. 'No. Just a bit lost and lonely at the moment—probably quite natural for a mother of an only child. Uh—something's burning.'

She turned back to the stove with a smothered exclamation and rescued the bacon.

'Twelve o'clock suit you, Ellie?'

'I haven't agreed to go.'

She heard him get up as she cracked two eggs and

added them to the pan and put some toast on. And the little hairs on the back of her neck rose, indicating he was standing behind her. The next moment the spatula was removed from her fingers and he turned her to face him.

'Brett!' she protested.

'Ellie,' he replied, 'I don't intend to take no for an answer.'

'You can't force me to go to lunch with you!'

'There is an alternative,' he said softly. His gaze roamed over her flushed face and the spot at the base of her throat where he had kissed her so pleasurably. 'As an antidote to being lost and lonely, perhaps even having a slightly sore head from a rather generous intake of champagne yesterday, some really rousing sex can work wonders.'

'D-don't touch me,' she stammered.

He smiled, the most enigmatic smile she'd ever seen. 'How about lunch, then?'

'All right,' she said rapidly, 'but I'll probably be very annoyed about it!'

'We'll see.' He handed her back the spatula and, adding insult to injury, dropped the lightest kiss on the top of her head. 'Go to it, Mrs Beeton.'

He took her to a seafood restaurant across the river— and it was impossible to remain annoyed.

They made the crossing in one of the river cats, the fast catamaran ferries that plied the Brisbane River, and were a treat not only as a means of getting from A to B but as a way of experiencing one of Brisbane's great resources, its river.

In fact, Ellie noted as they sat in the sun and skimmed over the water, the way Brett looked around it was as if he were taking his home town in through his pores, and loving it.

'A bit different from the Congo?' she said.

'A lot different.'

'You must have had some good times there, though,' she suggested.

'I had some great times and I met some great people, but home's nice.'

Ellie sighed suddenly.

He looked a question at her.

'I love Brisbane too,' she said ruefully. 'It's just that I had great plans to backpack my way around the world before I reached thirty.'

'You may find that the delay only means you'll be able to do it in more comfort.'

'I may need to find myself a rich husband,' she said thoughtlessly.

He raised an eyebrow but said, 'You're looking very chic, Ms Madigan.'

Ellie glanced down at her outfit, a white, summery, sleeveless tunic top over a three-quarter-length gathered cinnamon skirt and matching sandals. She always liked the swirl of the skirt around her legs and she had a lovely straw hat with a wide brim on. 'Thank you. You don't look too bad yourself.'

She said it lightly, as a throwaway line, but it was all too true. With a breeze ruffling his dark hair and wearing a blue and white striped shirt, open at the throat, with his moleskins, he was extremely good-looking.

'Thank you!' He took her hand as the river cat docked. 'After you, ma'am.'

They sat on the restaurant's terrace beneath an umbrella overlooking the river and she refused a glass of wine in favour of a long, cool soft drink and ordered butterfly prawns. He ordered a beer and grilled schnapper.

'Not inclined to have some hair of the dog, Ellie?'

'No.' She looked rueful. 'I'm feeling fine now but I don't drink during the day because I need my wits about me, I guess. Not that Simon's here at the moment.'

He smiled. 'Is he such a handful—Simon?'

She wrinkled her nose. 'No more than any active ten-year-old boy, I suspect. He's actually pretty good.'

'You and he seem to have a great relationship.'

'Even though I may have missed out on backpacking my way around the world, I think it's helpful to be young enough to relate to your kids or—' she looked impish '—perhaps there'll always be a bit of kid in me.'

'You certainly don't look like the mother of ten-year-old.'

Ellie studied him through her lashes, then she said abruptly, 'You're still doing it, Brett, trying to massage my ego. But I can fight my own battles.'

He subjected her attractive outfit and immaculate grooming to another brief inspection.

'All right!' she said frustratedly, then had to laugh. 'I guess Chantal has put me on my mettle, such as it is. But the only person I'm concerned about feeling good about me *is* me, not *you* about me, if that makes sense.'

'Perfect sense,' he murmured, with a wicked glint of humour in his eyes. 'But before Chantal hit us, it had already occurred to me that there was almost a new you, Ellie, from the girl of Tom's time and even the last time we met. A much more vibrant, confident person. Being thirty becomes you, Elvira Madigan.'

It was so long since anyone had called her that, Ellie almost did a double take. By the time she'd realized she'd been named after a Danish tightrope walker who'd had an affair with a Swedish army officer with tragic consequences, she'd changed her name in her mind to Ellie, and had used it ever since.

Now she said, 'Don't remind me.'

He looked amused. 'I always thought it was rather attractive. But to get back to the you of now, I'm impressed, Ellie, and full of admiration for how you've coped with life. I know it can't have been easy.'

She stared into his eyes, then looked away with a slight shiver. 'You do what you have to, I guess, that's all. But it hasn't all been doom and gloom. I can't imagine life without Simon now, he brings me so much joy.' She smiled and sniffed.

'I'm glad,' he said simply.

Ellie frowned suddenly. 'Is that why you want to stay around us now—apart from Simon, of course? Because I'm a better person?'

'I didn't say that. As a matter of fact, the first time you intrigued me and it occurred to me that I'd like to sleep with you was when you were nineteen and the day I found out what your real name was.'

If her synapses had been tested recently they now flashed in collective disbelief. *'What?'*

He lay back in his chair. 'It's true. That name and something a little lost, embarrassed and lovely about you definitely prompted the thought.'

Ellie could only stare at him.

'I guess you're wondering why I've never mentioned it?' He raised an eyebrow at her.

'Yes. No.' She put a hand to her mouth. 'Why *didn't* you?'

He shrugged. 'First of all there was Tom. Then you were grieving for Tom and pregnant. And by the time

Simon was born I knew I'd be away for long periods and I doubted you'd got over Tom anyway.'

'So, what you're saying…' her voice was shaky '…is this. You'd thought about sleeping with me as opposed to falling in love with me? Just as it crossed your mind that Chantal was desirable but you could take it or leave it?'

'I'm saying the time hasn't been right to mention it, that's all,' he replied evenly. 'It's right now for more reasons than one. So that you know it isn't something that's jumped up out of the blue for me and—eleven years ago there was no Chantal or a stint in the Congo I was trying to readjust from.'

Ellie could only stare at him with her lips parted.

He smiled rather satanically and recommended that she eat her lunch before it got cold.

She blushed, and did as she was told. In fact she ate every morsel of her lunch in silence as a delaying tactic while she grappled with this revelation and how to handle it. But her thoughts were jumping like fleas, with a definite tendency to jump backwards rather than forwards.

She'd been so sure she'd never appealed to Brett in any way. But suddenly, and clear as a bell, she remembered the day Tom had let slip her real name to Brett Spencer.

She'd experienced her usual embarrassment—she'd worn her hair long in those days and to cover the embarrassment she'd taken her scrunchie off, combed her fingers through her hair, then gathered it back into the scrunchie. As she'd lowered her arms she'd become aware that Brett's gaze had still been on her, and for no reason she'd been able to think of she'd felt hot and bothered over more than her father's explanation that, once they had a daughter, he and her mother could never seem to get beyond the name Elvira to go with Madigan.

But all she'd been able to put that feeling down to was yet another reason for Brett Spencer to disapprove of her.

Now, though, it all fell into place as she remembered also that he'd said, surprisingly gently, it was a pretty name. And she dipped her last prawn into the tartar sauce and felt her heart soar like a bird…

Moments later it came tumbling down as she rinsed her fingers in the flower-studded bowl. Two or three years perhaps, but *eleven* years was an awfully long time to wait to do anything about the feeling that had come to him.

She picked up her glass and studied the river traffic. There were seagulls wheeling noisily above a trawler as it steamed up stream, and the bow of a trim little blue and white yacht rose and sank gently as it sailed through the trawler's wake.

Brett finished his fish and put his knife and fork together but she couldn't bring herself to meet his eyes. She couldn't, yet, work out what she'd be getting herself into if she admitted her true feelings to him. It was all so new, so…it was still pretty flimsy, she thought.

'I gather I've floored you, Ellie.'

She had to look at him at last. 'Perhaps,' she conceded. 'I had no idea.'

Their gazes clashed.

'Well?' he said softly.

Ellie felt her forehead bead with sweat as her pulses started to hammer and she had no doubt that at this point in time, at least, Brett was actively thinking of sleeping with her. It was there between them like an invisible conduit, allowing something in his gaze to arouse the most intimate sensations in her. It was like being caressed mentally and not a whole lot different from the real thing—and this time she had no magazine to hide behind as these powerful sensations raced through her.

She moved restlessly as it became plain she'd aroused some quizzical amusement across the table. 'Look, I don't know what to say! I…it…it may be amusing for you, but it's not for me.'

'My apologies, I didn't mean to laugh at you. But…' he paused and frowned '…your reaction seemed to suggest it was out of the question for you to be found attractive and desirable.'

'By you, yes,' she conceded.

'Is that because you never thought about me in the same way—discounting recent times?'

She swallowed and frantically tried to organise her thoughts. 'No,' she said rather bleakly, at last. 'But that may only place me in the same category as—' she gestured '—the waitress who served us. What I mean to say is it could be an occupational hazard for most women who cross your path. There is a huge distinction between that and…really being in love with someone, however.'

'It all has to start somewhere, though.'

'Only a man could say that!' She eyed him darkly.

He grinned. 'You're wrong. It was said to me by a woman very recently as it happens.'

She blinked.

'Chantal Jones,' he supplied. 'Your sister-at-arms.'

A reluctant smile tugged at Ellie's lips. 'She's not really, and, forgive me, but I wouldn't say you've completely cured yourself of her yet, Brett, but—start what?'

He sat back. 'I wasn't suggesting that you and I leap straight into bed, Ellie. Merely that we consider the future and the possibilities.'

It was like having cold water dashed over her and there was nothing she could do to hide it.

She said stiffly, 'I think I'd like to go home now.'

'This time I've offended you.'

She didn't answer; she switched her gaze to the river, then looked at her watch. 'I think there's a ferry due shortly.'

'Wouldn't you like some coffee?'

'No, thank you. And thanks for lunch but I've got that kite to finish off so I really ought to get home—' She stopped abruptly and closed her eyes briefly.

At the same time someone walked up to the table, a svelte, attractive brunette, saying, 'Brett Spencer—is it really you?'

He stood up. 'Delia Saunders—is it really you?' And an enthusiastic reunion followed.

'But I'm no longer Delia Saunders, Brett! I married Archie McKinnon about three years ago, don't know why I waited so long,' Delia said humorously. 'We're deliriously happy!'

'Congratulations, I always thought you and Archie were made for each other! Delia, this is Ellie.'

Delia did a speedy reconnaissance and must have liked what she saw because she sat down excitedly. 'This is so fortuitous,' she said. 'It's our third wedding anniversary next weekend and we're having a party. Do please come, both of you!'

'Why not?' Brett said. 'Thank you, Delia.'

'I'm not going,' Ellie said to the river.

'Why didn't you say so at the time?'

Ellie watched the wake of the river cat for a long moment, then tossed him an irony-laden glance. 'How—

without making a complete fool of myself? It was hard enough to know what to say at all.'

He shrugged. 'Delia always gives wonderful parties.'

'That's not the point. Going out and about as a couple is—a complication we don't need, surely?'

'Why?'

'Brett, you're being obtuse—or something,' she accused.

He grinned wickedly. 'It would be a good way of getting to know another facet of each other, wouldn't you agree?'

'I'm not sure that's what we should be doing or will be doing. I'm not sure at all,' she said a little bleakly.

'Well, think about it,' he suggested. 'In the meantime do you mind if I drop you off at home? I need to do a few things in town.'

Think about it, Ellie repeated in her mind as she let herself into the quiet house.

And was surprised to discover she felt like screaming again and shouting with a mixture of frustration and disbelief. What, precisely, did he have in mind? An affair? True, there'd been that moment when things had got electric between them. But despite his protestations of innocence he must have created some electricity for Chantal—quite possibly he was able to turn it on and off like a tap!

But how much of the real Brett Spencer did she know? Enough to make an informed decision on the subject of taking the quantum leap into his bed?

'There's something here that doesn't gel,' she said to herself, and with a sigh got to work on her kite.

CHAPTER FIVE

SIMON came home late on Sunday afternoon looking tanned and fit and glowing with enthusiasm. Causing Ellie to say with a trace of irony, after she'd welcomed him with open arms, that for such an avowed *away-from-nature* freak his enthusiasm for camping was a little surprising.

'It's all in the company, Mum! We had a ball, midnight feasts, we played poker and I got to abseil down a cliff!'

She raised her eyebrows.

'Just as well you weren't there,' he said with a cheeky grin. 'You'd have been having kittens.'

Ellie upended his bag on the kitchen floor to find every piece of clothing mud-stained and damp. 'Glory be,' she murmured. 'Did it rain a lot up there?'

'Nope, not a drop!'

'So?' She picked up a T-shirt gingerly.

'There was this fantastic waterhole. We used to pretend we were hippos and sing that song.'

'"Mud, mud, glorious mud?"'

'Yep.' Simon dissolved into laughter.

'You are aware that you've probably ruined all these clothes?'

'No way,' he said blithely. 'You're brilliant at getting out stains!'

'I just hope your faith in her isn't misplaced,' Brett said, coming into the kitchen and eyeing the mound of clothes ruefully. 'But it's good to have you back, mate.'

'Just between you and me, it's good to be back,' Simon said and cocked an eye in Ellie's direction. 'She been handling things OK?'

'Simon,' Ellie said severely.

'She had a couple of lonely days,' Brett answered, 'but I kept an eye on her and I took her out to lunch yesterday.'

Ellie put her hands on her hips. 'Would you two stop discussing me as if I wasn't right here in this kitchen— or only about ten myself?'

Simon came over to her and put his arms around her waist. 'Remember when you used to read me Winnie the Pooh years ago? And James James Morrison Morrison Weatherby George Dupree who took great care of his mother although he was only three? I wouldn't have gone on this camp if I hadn't thought I was leaving you in good hands—you've got to take care of the people you love!' He hugged her.

For some reason as Ellie's eyes met Brett's over the top of Simon's head she disturbed a narrowed thoughtful look in his. Then the moment broke, Simon moved away from her and announced that he was starving.

'Some things never change,' she said wryly. 'Well—'

'Let's have a barbecue,' Brett suggested. 'Why don't you sit outside and leave it all to us, Ellie? I reckon you deserve a break.'

'Oh, I don't mind—'

'Do as you're told, Mum,' Simon said firmly.

'Talk about having not one but two bossy males in the house,' she marvelled, and looked around her kitchen a little apprehensively.

'We'll also clean up,' Brett murmured, interpreting her look accurately. 'Off you go. I'll bring you a drink.'

*   *   *

To their credit, while they kept it simple, it wasn't a bad barbecue the two men in her life presented.

Brett lit the fire and grilled sausages, steak and onions, at the same time instructing Simon in the finer arts of barbecuing. And between them they concocted new potatoes in their jackets brushed with melted garlic butter and sprinkled with chopped parsley; and sliced tomato drizzled with dressing and topped with basil.

'I'm impressed,' she said. 'I may be able to hand the kitchen over to you two completely!'

Simon and Brett exchanged identical glances—expressions of extreme reluctance that made her laugh softly. 'Don't worry, only teasing. Thanks, guys!' She raised her glass to them. 'You've done good.'

They ate leisurely, enjoying the evening and the aroma of wood smoke lingering on the air although there were distant flashes of lightning on the horizon.

Then out of the blue Simon said, 'What school did my dad go to, Mum?'

For a moment Ellie was floored and it was Brett who answered. He named a famous private school and added that it was his old school too.

'Gosh! My best friend, Martie Webster's dad went there, and Martie's going when he gets to high school. Will I be able to, Mum?'

Ellie hesitated. 'I don't think so, Simon. It's the kind of school you probably need to have your name put down for when you're born. But...' she paused as his face fell '...you must have other friends who are going to the local high school?'

He shrugged. 'I guess so. I just thought it would be nice to go to my dad's old school. And it would be nice to know a bit more about him.'

'You look a lot like him, Simon,' Brett said easily.

'And did you know he lived in this house? He lost his mother and father when he was thirteen so he came to us.'

Simon looked around interestedly. 'Could you tell me about that?'

'Sure.' Brett stood up. 'Let's do the dishes at the same time. And I guess your mum would like a cup of coffee.'

They left Ellie on the terrace—prey to some conflicting emotions. An ache in her heart because the time had finally come for Simon to think about his father. She'd tried to prepare herself as well as she could for the inevitable questions and had fallen at the first fence—not even remembering what school Tom had been to. But the most conflicting emotion was—how much more hero worship would Brett Spencer earn as the one person Simon could talk to about Tom?

Coffee came but Simon decided to take himself to bed.

He shook his head as he yawned mightily and said quaintly, 'It's all that fresh air! Night, Mum.' He kissed her and took himself off.

Brett sat down.

'What...what did you tell him?' Ellie asked.

'How good Tom used to be at cricket, how he'd always been fascinated by building bridges and roads, how he was the only person I ever knew who could imitate a fish perfectly—that kind of thing.'

'And polo? I've only ever told him it was a riding accident.'

Brett seemed to go quite still for a moment. Then he said, barely audibly, 'No. I didn't mention polo. About his schooling, Ellie?'

She sighed and thought for a bit. Tom's old school had an excellent academic as well as sporting record, not to mention conferring considerable status in the old-school-tie stakes. 'There's no way I could afford it even if I could get him in.'

'I could.'

It was Ellie's turn to go still. Then she said awkwardly, 'I know you could afford it but what about the waiting list? I'm sure there is one.'

He stared at her for a long moment. 'There is, but there are also places for old boys' sons.'

'That might have helped if Tom and I had been married but we weren't,' she said, 'so I don't suppose it applies. And I couldn't accept any more financial help from you, Brett.'

'I was talking about—as my son.'

Ellie blinked rapidly. 'You mean…?'

'If we got married, Ellie, I could get Simon into the school his father went to and his best friend is going to, but those aren't the only reasons—it's a damn good school and he has so much potential, he deserves it.'

'Brett,' she whispered, 'I can't believe this!'

'Why not?' he asked impatiently.

'Is there…' she hesitated and made herself think as clearly as she could '…is there something that's made you decide you need a wife? And since I'm—virtually—in place, so to speak, I might as well be it?'

'No. I wouldn't put it like that.' He paused and narrowed his eyes. 'But we are "in place". We're virtually living a phantom marriage right now. And the reason we got here was because we both have the same person's interests very much at heart. That has never changed. Only it's got more critical now, and up until now I've had the easy part.' He paused again. 'I also have Simon's blessing.'

'How?'

'He saw us that night.'

'I know but...' She was lost for words.

'He came to me the next morning very much man-to-man and explained how it had happened. He also gave me to understand I had his blessing, and he gave me some advice.'

'I don't believe it!' But it was more out of sheer frustration that she said it—she could quite believe it of Simon.

'When did he tell you?' Brett enquired.

'The morning he rang from camp. Advice?' she repeated with deep misgiving. 'What *kind* of advice?'

'He explained that in his opinion you were a very cautious person, you didn't take easily to new ideas and it was all in the handling.'

Ellie all but choked.

'He is your son,' Brett commented wryly.

'I just hope you...didn't get his hopes up, Brett Spencer!'

He watched her for a moment. 'I've discovered that with Simon there are times when you don't need to say much. So I was essentially noncommittal. Although I think I gave him to understand that he needn't play an active role in any negotiations between you and I.'

'Brett, has it occurred to you that you seem to spend a lot of time giving people advice they don't take?'

He raised an eyebrow at her.

'Well, there's Chantal Jones, still more than convinced you're the right man for her, and Simon—' She broke off and bit her lip.

'He gave you some advice despite my advice?' Brett suggested wryly. 'Even his blessing perhaps?'

Ellie was silent, in itself a dead give away.

'There you go, then,' Brett said. 'As for the romantic

side of things, that's also "in place", wouldn't you say?' There was more than a tinge of irony in his grey eyes.

She shivered suddenly. 'Romance is one thing, love is another and that's what I need. It's been too long and hard a road to…compromise.'

'Love can come and go,' he said evenly. 'It could even be the most misunderstood emotion of all. But what might make it prosper is a common goal such as providing a child with a stable family life.'

She flinched this time.

He saw it and added, 'As a matter of fact I not only have Simon's best interests at heart, but yours as well. Can you honestly tell me, Ellie, that a stable married life to me wouldn't be a better bet than a succession of— artists, musicians and back-to-nature freaks?'

She was silent, feeling hurt and foolish, and, because of it, on the defensive but what came next wiped the floor with her pride.

'Can you honestly say—' he sat forward '—that certain emotions the long, hard road froze are not clamouring for expression now? Eleven years is a long time to clamp down on wanting to…live and love.'

She closed her eyes.

'In that sense,' he went on quietly, 'I am a much better bet than the choices you've made up to now.'

He saw it in her eyes as her lashes fluttered up, as if a shutter had come down, and knew he'd gone too far and hurt her pride. But he couldn't seem to help himself. In fact it was worse. He didn't care that he couldn't help himself. Why? Because he'd never before acknowledged to himself how hard he'd had to clamp down on the interest she'd aroused in him all those years ago? The interest that had caused him to wonder about his best friend's girl in ways that he shouldn't have. That interest and curiosity about her essence as a woman...

Had it then become habit, he wondered, that clamping down? Helped along by a streak of guilt because he'd thought of her the way he had while she'd been Tom's girl? Although one thing had never changed. He had always been determined to do as much for Tom King's son as he could.

She drained her coffee and stood up. 'On the other hand, I think Chantal is a much better bet for you, Brett.'

'Ellie.' His voice was suddenly hard. 'I have no intention of letting Tom's son be subjected to your dubious choice in men.'

She gasped as he got up and towered over her looking determined enough to do anything. But she stood her ground and paid the price. He took her in his arms.

'Brett, this is not what I would have believed of you,' she said stiffly.

A flicker of amusement chased through his eyes. 'Why not? I'm a man and I've been wanting to kiss you for eleven years.'

'No, you haven't,' she contradicted. 'It may have crossed your mind once or twice eleven years ago, that's all.'

'It not only crossed my mind, I did it a few *days* ago.' His words were barely audible but they came across to her with a comprehensive glance of an intensity that shook her a little. Then he added with another flicker of humour, 'You may be able to turn these things on and off like a tap; I can't.'

Ellie's mouth fell open as his words mirrored what she'd mentally accused him of in relation to Chantal.

'That's struck a chord?' he said slowly.

She closed her mouth with a click.

'As in suspecting…me of it?' he hazarded.

She went crimson and he started to laugh softly. 'Well, well, Ms Madigan,' he drawled, 'my reputation if nothing else is at stake here. I think I need to prove you wrong!'

'Reputation—or ego?'

'Could be both,' he said blandly. 'There's only one way to find out—' He stopped as a flash of lightning right above them lit the night, then a crack of thunder followed.

Ellie shivered and clutched at him.

'Scared,' he said softly and folded her closer.

'Mmm…' She flinched at another flash of lightning. 'Brett, let's get inside!'

'OK.' He picked her up as if she were a feather and carried her into the lounge as the first raindrops fell like bullets. 'Would you like to check on Simon?' he suggested as he put her on her feet.

'Yes! Although he doesn't mind storms.'

'I'll do it, you sit down.'

She sank onto the settee and waited until he came back.

'He's fine,' he said a few minutes later, sitting down beside her. 'He's out like a light. Does he always take *Guinness World Records* to bed?' And he took her in his arms as if it was the most natural thing in the world.

She smiled. 'Always. It's his great ambition to be in it one day, he just hasn't decided what for.' And, as if the cork on the bottle of her emotions had suddenly popped, there were tears in her eyes although she was still smiling. She dashed at them impatiently. 'Sorry, don't know what's got into me.'

'Oh, Ellie,' he said on a breath, and started to kiss her.

When he stopped, she was feeling far from tearful. Warm, cherished, drowsy and completely relaxed. And completely at home. In fact she fell asleep in his arms.

He looked down at her face nestled against his shoulder, and could feel her gentle curves against him, and found himself feeling protective.

He laid his head back, careful not to disturb her, and examined with some surprise what had transpired this evening. He had actually articulated the thought that had come to him several times down the years—that they get married for Simon's sake. Little to know that he was now questioning how much of it had to do with Simon, and questioning his difficulty in seeing past marrying her for all the wrong reasons. Although, he reflected with a tightening of his mouth, there was one wrong reason she didn't even know about.

But if he was questioning his motives, what of hers?

He looked down at her sleeping so peacefully in his arms.

There was no doubt she responded to him physically but would she, could she fall in love again? With him? Because, he acknowledged, unless they got it right, all other considerations aside, they might not benefit Simon at all. In other words, he would have to go out of his way to make Simon's mother happy, if that was what he wanted to achieve for Simon himself.

He looked down at Ellie again as she moved slightly but didn't wake. And there was, of course, his thoughts ran on, his part in Tom King's son, a boy he was growing more attached to by the day, being fatherless...

Ellie woke up in her bed the next morning, still fully clothed although her shoes had been removed.

She sat up suddenly, then it all fell into place. But a

glance at her bedside clock saw her scatter bedclothes left, right and centre; she'd slept in and had a bare half-hour to get Simon off to school and herself off to work.

But Brett was already up and Simon was dressed and ready for school, calmly eating his cereal and fruit as she flew into the kitchen, still buttoning up her blouse.

She skidded to a stop, eyed the situation and said lamely, 'Oh.'

'Hi, Mum! You look a bit frazzled.'

And Brett, whom she had no idea how to face, put a cup of tea down in her place at the table with a murmured greeting.

'Thanks.' She slid into her chair and sipped the tea gratefully. She was never much good for anything until she'd had a cup of tea in the morning. 'Uh…how come you two are up so bright and early?'

'We've been for a jog and a swim,' Simon said virtuously. 'You should try it.'

'I…maybe I will one day.'

Brett sat down. He wore his usual attire for work, moleskins and a checked shirt, and as usual he looked alert and altogether too much man for any woman to have to cope with at that time of the day. 'Guys,' he said casually, 'I have to go away for a few days. Think you'll manage without me?'

'Sure.'

'Definitely!'

Simon and Ellie spoke at the same time with Ellie being the most emphatic of the two and Brett flicked her a quizzical little look.

'Where to?' Simon enquired.

'A board meeting of a company I'm involved with in Sydney. I'd actually forgotten about it until I got a call from someone last night. And while I'm down there I have a few other things to do but I'll be back on Thursday.'

Ellie said airily, 'Not a problem. We're used to being on our own, aren't we, kid?'

Simon saluted her. 'You gotta admit it's nice to have a man around the place, though, Mum.'

'Oh, I do—lunch!' Ellie got up distractedly.

'All taken care of,' Brett said. 'And I'll drop Simon off at school—when you're ready, mate.'

'I'll just clean my teeth. Meet you in the car! Bye, Mum!'

Brett waited until Simon was out of earshot, then he came over to where Ellie was standing looking shell-shocked. 'I'm sorry about this,' he said quietly. 'I did forget all about it.'

'That's OK.'

'Is it?' There was a humorous little glint in his eyes.

She twisted her hands together. 'About last night.'

He raised an eyebrow. 'Nothing happened—that you weren't aware of.'

She bit her lip. 'I didn't mean that. But I…got a bit carried away again.'

'No, Ellie, we got carried away again. It's almost becoming a habit with us.'

She said bravely, 'What about the rest of it?'

'Maybe…' he paused '…a few days apart isn't such a bad idea. To get things into perspective?'

A flash of amusement made the golden flecks in her eyes more noticeable. 'You're suggesting I "think" about it?'

A cheeky tiddly-pom sounded on the hooter of Brett's Range Rover, courtesy of Simon.

'I did hesitate to use that word,' he conceded gravely, 'in case you felt like screaming. But—why not?'

Ellie took a breath. 'All right, but I'm not promising anything,' she warned.

'Of course you're not!' he said bracingly. 'In the meantime, your son is getting impatient. So, *hasta luego, muchacha*!'

Ellie looked surprised, then her lips quivered. 'And the same to you, *muchacho*.'

Unfortunately, the next few days proved to be incredibly busy as not one but two colleagues were laid low by a gastric bug doing the rounds, thereby doubling her workload. It was a busy week for Simon as well with the school swimming carnival approaching, the end of year school play and the cricket season was under way.

Therefore he needed an enormous amount—or so it sometimes felt—of transporting to and from the school pool, the school hall, the cricket field, not to mention the making of his costume for the play—he was to be a trooper in a Ned Kelly saga.

'I suppose it could have been worse,' Ellie muttered to herself one evening. 'He could have been Ned Kelly—then I'd have had to come up with a tin and metal costume.'

'I tried out for Ned Kelly,' Simon commented, overhearing her. 'But I'm not so sure he was the hero everyone seems to think he was.'

'He was a bush ranger,' Ellie agreed. 'But circumstances, they claim, made him one.' She put down the jacket she was sewing buttons onto and concentrated more closely on what Simon had said. 'Did you knock back being Ned Kelly? Because you're not sure he was such a hero?'

'Yep.'

'You didn't tell me that!'

'I was afraid you'd accuse me of un-Australian inclinations.'

Ellie blinked, then started to laugh. 'You are a character, Simon. To be honest, I've never felt quite comfortable with Ned Kelly myself. So I'm glad you decided to stay on the side of the law.'

Later, however, on her own and getting ready for bed, Ellie reflected that, for ten, Simon was unusually perceptive and enquiring of mind. Which brought her face to face with the issue of his schooling and the short hop to the issue of marrying Brett Spencer.

She changed into a cotton-knit nightshirt and stretched wearily before she climbed into bed and pulled a pillow into her arms for comfort. But, tired as she was, her imagination took wings. It would be no penance to take Brett into her arms night after night, it would be sheer bliss, she thought, and moved restlessly as her body reacted to her thoughts.

And she knew enough now to know that it would be no penance for him to make love to her. But forever? she wondered. Or, would it one day turn to duty and, if so, how could she bear that?

Yet, are there *forevers* for anyone? she wondered. And what about Chantal Jones? Wasn't he attracted to her as well?

The next morning, she had a later start, thanks to her laid-low colleagues being back at work, and the subject of Chantal came up in the form of Dan paying her a visit. A chastened, supremely embarrassed Dan.

'You don't have to explain,' she said as she poured him a cup of coffee and told him to sit down. 'I quite understand.'

'I do, Ellie,' he insisted. 'I don't know what came over me!'

Ellie studied his earnest expression. 'Dan,' she said slowly, 'I hope you aren't still hoping that you and I—'

'Ellie—'

'No, listen to me, Dan, I'm not for you and that's the way things are.'

'I just didn't want you thinking badly of me. But I guess most men would get in a bit of a flutter over someone like Chantal,' he said slowly. 'I mean—it doesn't really mean anything and, anyway, heaven alone knows who the right guy is for her, but I'm sure it wouldn't be me.'

Ellie grimaced inwardly at these revealing, less-than-flattering sentiments, did he but know it, but she returned resolutely, although obliquely, to the main issue. 'How much leave have you got left, Dan?'

'Two weeks.'

'Good, because there's no reason on earth that you mightn't be just the right guy for Chantal and you've got a bit of time to put it to the test.'

He stared at her with his mouth open. 'Ellie—'

'Dan, really,' she said firmly, '*I'm* not for you. But you'll never know about Chantal unless you give it a try.'

'How…?' He cleared his throat. 'How would you go about it? If you were me?'

'I think,' Ellie said seriously, and thought rapidly at the same time as she controlled an insane desire to laugh, 'persistence might be the key with Chantal. And I think she might like a good time—you do know she's…a dancer?' There was sudden anxiety in Ellie's eyes.

'Yes—remember, she told us about the revue she's in?'

Ellie relaxed although she couldn't remember if the word 'topless' had featured. 'Of course. But I think she would also appreciate a fairly subtle approach—keep trying, in other words, but don't be too obvious.'

Dan sat up, looking like a new man. 'I'll do it! But just remember, Ellie, if ever you need a friend, give me a call.'

Her gaze softened. 'Thanks, Dan.'

When he'd left, she put her hand to her mouth and wondered wildly what she'd let him in for, not to mention Chantal. Well, she was pretty sure Chantal could take care of herself but... She heaved a sigh and wondered instead what Brett would make of her meddling.

Then she stood up and tossed her head. Who gave a damn? They were both grown men.

'So?'

It was Friday again, Brett had been delayed in Sydney and he'd got home just in time for dinner. Simon had had his earlier and was at a rehearsal.

And Ellie had blinked when he'd come in the back door. She'd never seen him so formally dressed, in a dark suit, a grey and white pinstriped shirt, a charcoal and green tie, and he'd taken her breath away.

He'd shed his jacket and tie and sat down at the kitchen table where she'd just started her dinner—home-made lasagne—and asked his one-word question.

'Uh...hi!' Ellie said, and after an uncertain start rushed on, 'I hope you made sure that no woman sitting next to you switched overnight bags.'

He glanced at the bag he'd dropped to the floor wryly. 'No chance of that. She was eighty if she was a day.'

'Oh, I wouldn't get too blasé, Brett.' She bit her lip and wondered where she was coming from—out to make him aware of how attractive he was? Or talking from fright because of the effect he'd had on her and because she hadn't decided anything?

'So?' he said again. 'How's it going?'

She breathed a discreet sigh of relief. 'Fine. Well, incredibly busy.'

He served himself some lasagne. 'How so?'

She explained, causing him to look at her rather narrowly, then get up and open a bottle of wine.

And her eyes widened as he placed a glass beside her plate and murmured, 'You look as if you could do with it.'

'How am I looking?'

He studied her simple apple-green top and cargo shorts, then her face and eyes. 'A bit stressed out. What you need is some relaxation. Such as Delia's party tomorrow night.'

Ellie grimaced. 'I'd forgotten all about it.'

'I don't know much about women,' Brett Spencer said then with a most wicked little glint in his grey eyes, 'but as an antidote to stress mightn't all the trappings of a party help?'

'What exactly do you mean by all the trappings?'

He shrugged. 'A new dress, a visit to the beauty parlour perhaps, a lazy afternoon—I'll do all Simon's transporting—then a night of good food, good music and a bit of fun?'

Ellie closed her eyes and visualized it all even though she knew that the feminist part of her soul should be outraged, and that Brett Spencer knew too much about women for *her* good.

'There'll have to be explanations of why we're sharing the same house—I don't think I could cope,' she said simply.

'Why don't you leave all that up to me?'

'But what…how will you explain it? I mean, then we have to go into whose child Simon is—don't you see how difficult it all is for me?'

He shrugged. 'Ellie, this will not be the Spanish Inquisition. We don't have to say a word on any of those subjects. But it so happens that Delia has a child from an earlier relationship.'

'Oh!'

He smiled slightly. 'The world has moved on from the days when that kind of thing was taboo, Ellie.'

'I know that, but the biggest problem of all,' she soldiered on, 'is going out as a couple when nothing is resolved between us. You seem to think it can be on the basis of two kisses, I don't—'

'Two very pleasurable kisses.'

'Maybe.' She moved restlessly, then squared her shoulders with more spirit than she actually felt.

'What exactly are you looking for, Ellie?' he said slowly. 'A declaration of undying love from me?'

'Of course not.'

His eyes flickered and she had the sensation of being on dangerous ground, although she didn't exactly know why. She swallowed and pushed her plate away frustratedly.

'Look, you're making a mountain out of a molehill. But if you are still divided on the benefits of marrying me…' he paused and eyed her until she started to colour '…the more we see of each other in different situations, the more it might help you to make an informed judgement.'

'Why do I get the feeling that's another twisted bit of logic?' she murmured and got up to clear the dishes.

But he got up too and detained her with a hand on

her wrist. 'We could always stay at home and carry on where we left off the other night,' he said softly, and glanced significantly down at her breasts beneath the apple green top.

And his lips twisted into an absent smile as her nipples started to push against the cotton knit.

'I'd appreciate it if you didn't...do this to me,' she said with an effort.

He raised an eyebrow. 'But I haven't done a thing, Ellie.'

'You... Let me go, please, Brett,' she said, even more hotly embarrassed.

'Will you come to the party?' He caressed the soft skin on her inner wrist with his fingers.

'That's blackmail...'

'Yep. But look at it this way, we wouldn't be on our own.' His eyes danced with sheer devilry.

'Oh, all right! But I could be—'

'Don't say it, I can guess,' he drawled. 'Be very annoyed about it?'

'Well, I could!' She stopped as the phone rang. 'That'll be Simon. He took my mobile so he could ring when the rehearsal was over.'

'I'll go and get him,' Brett said. 'While you work on your sense of grievance.' He raised her wrist to his lips and kissed the back of her hand.

CHAPTER SIX

BRETT was already out when Ellie left her bedroom the next morning but there was a note on the fridge for her saying that he'd consulted with Simon and they'd organised their day so she was a free agent.

And despite all her misgivings she took herself out to do all the things he'd recommended.

She had a facial and a manicure, got her hair done, then went to shop for something to wear. Delia had told her—what seemed like an eternity ago now—that the party would be chic casual. And she finally found just the right outfit. The top was in the latest fashion, a deep rose-pink, while the skirt was a light, airy material over a lining, white with rose-pink flowers on it. About an inch of her midriff was bare where the top ended and the skirt began. And she found an elegant pair of matching pink high-heeled sandals.

Then, on a bizarre impulse, she bought herself some new lingerie, silk and lace and light as a feather and including a gossamer nightgown and robe in a pale silvery grey trimmed with ice-coloured lace. She also splurged on new cosmetics, thereby blowing all the hard-earned extra money the week had brought her and some more.

'Wow!' Simon stared at her. 'You look stunning!'

'Thank you, young man,' Ellie said seriously. 'I take that as a great compliment. Have you got everything?'

He was going to spend the night with Martie Webster who lived a few houses away; it was a baby-sitting arrangement Ellie and Martie's parents had shared for years.

'Think so. OK, have fun!' He hugged her and took off, only to come running back for the container of Anzac cookies she'd baked. 'And don't do anything I wouldn't!' he added with a cheeky grin.

'Why do I get the feeling there's a *lot* of role reversal going on in this house?' she asked the empty kitchen.

Brett strolled in. 'Role reversal?'

'I feel just like James James Morrison Morrison Weatherby George Dupree's mother,' she told him. 'Mind you, let's hope I don't get lost like she did.'

'I...feel I've missed the boat somewhere along the line,' he said ruefully.

'Funnily enough, so do I!' Ellie said with irony. 'In your case I wouldn't worry about it.'

He blinked, then shook his head. 'One thing I do know, you're looking good enough to eat.' His gaze dwelt on the satiny skin of her bare shoulder and her slim outline in her new outfit; her shining cloud of curls in their elegant bob, the tiny gold rings she wore in her ears and the perfection of her make-up; her glossy lips...

'Yes, well—' Ellie turned away rather hurriedly and picked up her purse '—let's go.'

'In case...we get a little carried away again?' he postulated.

She turned back and said tartly, 'Brett Spencer, sheer pride has rendered me into cast iron!'

He laughed softly. 'Unfortunately, the same couldn't be said of me.' He picked up his car keys. 'So, you're right, let's go.'

As a conversation killer, his last comment worked well all the way out to Raby Bay, but he put on a favourite classical CD of hers, and she relaxed to the music and the lack of conversation didn't seem to be a problem. Although it did occur to her that they had similar taste in music.

As he nosed the magenta Range Rover, which Simon so desired to learn to drive, into the kerb beside a brightly lit house, Ellie stared out of the window and suffered another bout of nerves.

But Brett got out and came round to open her door and give her his hand to descend the steep step to the ground. And she walked up the path beside him but stopped abruptly a few paces from the front door.

He turned to her with a raised eyebrow.

'I won't know a soul.'

'Ellie—' he took her hand '—you have me.' And he dropped a light kiss on her hair. At the same time the front door swung open and Delia called a greeting.

There were about fifty people at Delia and Archie McKinnon's anniversary party, which turned out to be a very up-market barbecue on their waterfront terrace. And while quite a few of them knew Brett, they were so out of touch with him that her place in his life and her background went completely unremarked.

And she started to enjoy herself. The canapés were excellent, the wine flowed, the background music appealed to her and the conversation was stimulating. Archie McKinnon, a barrister, was very tall and thin and had a brilliant sense of humour and both he and Delia went out of their way to make Ellie feel welcome. Archie, it also turned out, had a passion for flying kites.

Then a late guest arrived; Gemma Arden, Brett's lawyer. As Ellie's only contact with Brett for a number of years, she'd had quite a bit to do with Ellie and they'd become friends.

'This is a pleasant surprise!' Gemma said warmly. 'How's Simon?'

'Fine, thank you!'

'And how…' Gemma looked around and lowered her voice, although Brett was helping Archie at the barbecue '…is our mutual friend coping with the rigours of civilization?'

A smile trembled on Ellie's lips. 'I don't think it's that easy, to be honest. It…may even have given him some strange ideas.'

Gemma's intelligent eyes glinted a question. 'Such as?'

Ellie grimaced and sipped some wine, regretting what she'd said.

'I was at university with Brett,' Gemma said quietly, 'and I'm not only his lawyer, we've been friends for years, so why don't you and I have lunch one day, Ellie? I also feel as if you and I are friends but you're right, this probably isn't the time or the place to discuss things—if you would like to?'

'I would,' Ellie said, making a sudden decision.

As they settled on Monday at twelve noon the main course was served. Reef and beef kebabs, grilled mushrooms, potatoes Idaho, ratatouille and a marvellous array of salads. If that was not enough there was pavlova, apple pie, fruit salad and ice cream to follow.

So, when couples began to dance and Brett looked a question at her, she was lulled by food, wine and good conversation and she couldn't resist the music. Also, Gemma had left the party—Ellie was sure she would have felt self-conscious about dancing with Brett in front of Gemma Arden.

The terrace lighting was turned off and only the underwater pool lights were left on, although lights did twinkle up and down the canal.

A jasmine creeper was perfuming the warm, sultry night air, and she felt good about herself—dressed right, not so much a single mother with all the burdens that encompassed, but an intelligent, sometimes witty person able to hold her own with a career others had found interesting. She felt as she hadn't felt for a long time, she discovered. Yes, she'd been to parties down the long road of single-motherhood, but not often and never as enjoyable as this.

So why not? she wondered as she started to dance with Brett. And realized that some of her new-found confidence had come from his presence. He had, mysteriously, contributed moral support.

Perhaps it was gratitude, perhaps it would have happened anyway—he was great to dance with—but being in his arms gradually unlocked that pure physical delight she'd felt the last time she'd been there until she stumbled suddenly.

He raised an eyebrow at her and stopped dancing.

'I don't do this very often,' she said awkwardly. 'I must be out of practice. I think I'd like to sit down.'

But he shook his head and drew her closer. 'You don't lie very well, Ellie.' And started to move to the rhythm again.

'Brett...' she said shakily. 'I thought this was what we were staying away from home to avoid?'

He glinted a look down at her that was so nakedly intimate her breath caught in her throat. A look that seemed to strip away her clothes and remove the two of them to some utterly private place where they could indulge their fascination with each other to the limit.

Then he said very softly, 'It doesn't seem to be working—and we can't spend the rest of our lives away from home. Should we make a discreet exit?'

She looked at him helplessly. 'I knew there was something wrong with your logic!'

'Logic?' he said wryly.

'You know what I mean.'

'The only logic that seems to apply is that we want each other, Ellie.'

'But I'm not ready to make that decision, Brett.'

He loosened his arms. 'Then let's stay,' he said dryly. 'Why miss out on a good party for a—possible lost cause?'

A flicker of anger lit her eyes. 'Saying something like that leads me to think you only have one thing in mind, Brett Spencer.'

'My dear Ellie,' he drawled, 'have you forgotten about Chantal Jones again?'

'No! Yes! I mean, oh, hell—she may not be very happy with me at the moment.'

'Why on earth not?' He stopped dancing.

Ellie explained briefly.

He stared down into her eyes for a long frozen moment, then his shoulders shook and he started to laugh. But what he said next really shook her. 'Do you know, that's exactly what I needed.'

'Needed? What do you mean?'

'I have to confess—' he started to dance again '—I've been battling a certain element of guilt in regard to Ms Jones. It's now gone.'

'Guilt?' Ellie stopped abruptly and frowned. 'Gone?'

'Yep.'

'How? Why?'

He shrugged. 'The thought of Dan Dawson falling out

of love with you and into love with her has—dissolved it.'

'Thank you,' she said with a tinge of bitterness, but then shook her head in a mystified kind of way. 'I still don't understand.'

'Look, I should never have let things go the way they did on the plane, especially as I had no intention of— following up.'

'Because she was a topless dancer?'

'No, well, I tried to tell myself that. But now Dan has succumbed, I don't feel so bad about myself.' He shrugged and looked rueful. 'She packs a powerful punch and we're only human.'

'Why didn't you have any intention of following up?' Ellie asked with a frown.

'I had someone called Elvira Madigan on my mind.'

Her eyes widened. 'Even then? But you hadn't seen me for five years!'

'I wasn't disappointed when I did.' He looked down at her. 'I should have thought,' he added, 'that much was obvious.'

An expression of such confusion crossed her face, he laughed softly and said, 'Still looking for logic, Ellie? When will you understand these matters don't respond to logic? They're there or they're not, they come and they go. But if you prefer to ignore them, be my guest.' And he swung her around with a flourish and brought her to a standstill. 'I don't know about you but I'm thirsty.'

'And I'm not the person who has just confessed to being attracted to two women at the same time—or did I get it wrong?' she said tautly.

'You got it dead right. But with Chantal it was only a prickle, just one of those things.'

'That still doesn't make me…feel very good,' she said desolately. 'Or present you in a very good light!' she added with more spirit.

He smiled lazily down at her. 'On the other hand I know a way to make you feel very good. What a dilemma for you, Elvira Madigan!' he said with a sardonic glint in his eye. 'But it's up to you.'

He released her, waited for a moment, but when there was only confusion in her eyes he took her hand and led her towards the drinks table.

They didn't stay until the bitter end but close to it, and the only good thing to come out of the rest of the party was that she sold a kite unseen to Archie McKinnon.

And while they maintained a friendly front for the rest of the evening, the tension in the Range Rover on the way home was tangible.

She glanced at him a couple of times beneath her lashes and saw a side of him she hadn't seen for the past couple of weeks. The hard side of Brett Spencer, and it made her shiver inwardly. Then she cautioned herself to take it into account should she ever decide to marry him. Although, she thought with a tremor, perhaps the offer of that privilege was about to be withdrawn?

She soon discovered it wasn't.

They went into the house by the front door and she hesitated in the hall. 'Goodnight. It was a nice party,' she said lamely.

He shoved his hands into his pockets and looked down at her impassively, his gaze lingering on the faint blue shadows beneath her eyes—and his mouth tightened for a moment. 'You look more stressed than you did when I came home. Look, forget Chantal and think about Simon. But most importantly, think of yourself.'

She swallowed.

'You know,' he continued, 'it's come as a bit of a surprise to find that you have such reservations about me, Ellie. It makes me wonder why you didn't move on years ago.'

Her eyes widened. 'If…if this seems like ingratitude, it's not that at all.'

'Blow gratitude,' he said roughly. 'It's the last thing I want. But it might be worthwhile remembering that I've always done what I could for you and Simon.'

There was sudden anguish in her eyes. 'I do remember that, Brett, but this is marriage you're talking about. It's—'

'It's something we can make heavy weather of, Ellie, or not. I'm in favour of ''not'' but I have no doubt it's what we should do. Go to bed,' he said, sounding weary himself, and he turned away.

Ellie got up late on Sunday morning, just as Simon returned from Martie's place. Brett was working in the study although he came out to get a cup of coffee.

'You guys look as if you had a late night,' Simon observed.

Ellie smiled feebly.

'Good party, Mum?'

'It was very good!' She tried to sound enthusiastic and winced inwardly as Simon shot her a piercing little look.

'Great food and great music,' Brett supplied as he poured his coffee. 'By the way, Archie rang a bit earlier. He wanted to know if he could come over and see your kites, Ellie.'

'Oh. Well, sure!'

'Good. I thought you'd say that so I invited them this

afternoon. Why don't we take some tea and stuff up to the park and give him a demonstration?'

'Them?'

'He's bringing Delia and Grace, Delia's daughter—she's about your age, Simon.'

'Ripper! I mean, I feel like flying kites in the park, although girls aren't much good at it usually. Which ones shall we take, Mum?'

'You choose, Simon,' Ellie said slowly and looked around the kitchen. 'I better do something for afternoon tea.'

'Ellie,' Brett said firmly, 'you don't have to get into *hausfrau* mode. I thought it would be a nice, relaxing break for you this afternoon.'

'Just one cake, perhaps?' she suggested.

'Let her,' Simon chimed in. 'She loves cooking, I think she finds it therioptic.'

'In that case—' Brett looked at Simon amusedly '—I bow to your greater knowledge of your mum, mate—if you meant therapeutic.'

'That's it!' Simon was unfazed. 'A bit like speech therapy only occupational. Takes her mind off things, in other words.'

'Would you two,' Ellie said dangerously, 'get out of my kitchen before I'm tempted to use a few choice words myself?'

'Uh-oh! A conniption coming on!' Simon warned. 'I'm gone—hey, Mum, don't forget how much I love gingerbread!' was his parting shot. Brett followed him out after casting Ellie a look full of wry humour.

It was a perfect day for kite-flying.

Clear skies, a light breeze and not too hot. The park had sweeping views of the river, and Ellie unpacked a minor feast on one of the tables. A gingerbread cake, wafer-like savoury sandwiches and pikelets with cream and strawberry jam. There were a flask of tea and soft drinks for the children.

'If I'd known you were going to go to so much trouble I'd have brought something myself,' Delia protested laughingly.

'She likes doing it,' Brett commented.

'Don't start,' Ellie warned and turned to Delia. 'This is only a fraction of the trouble you must have gone to yesterday and—' she grimaced '—I have to admit it's true. I enjoy it.'

'A woman of many talents!' Archie remarked, helping himself to a pikelet.

'How on earth you remain so thin is a complete mystery to me,' his wife said ruefully. 'He never stops eating!'

'I'm still growing,' Archie replied as he examined one of the kites and his eyes started to shine with enthusiasm. 'Can't you see the boy in me?'

They all laughed and Grace, who was as fair as her mother was dark and as pretty as a picture with shy blue eyes, took her stepfather's hand lovingly. 'Can you show me how to fly one?'

Simon stepped forward. 'I will, if you like. Why don't we try the butterfly? It's one of the easiest to handle and it looks great.'

They had two hours of glorious kite-flying. Ellie was in her element. She had on her cargo shorts and a floral blouse and as she demonstrated her expertise she felt as free as a bird, lithe and lissom—almost like a girl again but not only that. It was when she was flying the kites she'd designed and made that all sorts of fantasies claimed her. That one day she'd be acclaimed for her work with speech-impeded children; that one day she'd fly over the Serengeti in a balloon or sail the South Pacific or at least see the icy peaks of the Himalayas… That one day she'd see her son in *Guinness World Records* as was his dream.

Today, though, the fantasy went in a different direction. That one day she'd be the confident, slightly mysterious, ever fascinating woman Brett Spencer couldn't get enough of. As opposed, she thought as her kite soared, to the woman who ran his home efficiently and was already in place…

Several times she felt Brett's eyes on her, taking her in from her wind-tangled curls to her bare toes; once looking slightly amused as she and Archie discussed updraughts and down-draughts and the right wind velocity to get a kite to spin. But there was no way he could read her mind, she assured herself.

Two hours later she also realized with a pang that Simon had fallen in love for the very first time. Girls hadn't featured much in his life until now but Grace, after she'd got over her shyness and proved an apt pupil, had changed that.

And she was watching them frolicking without a care in the world with a lump in her throat.

'Those two have really hit it off,' Brett said from behind her.

She turned to him. 'Haven't they? I may no longer be the only woman in Simon's life.'

'Would that be so bad if you were the woman in my life?' he asked barely audibly.

Her eyes widened at the concept and his understanding of the situation, but she was saved from answering as Archie came up to tell them he would like to buy not one but two kites—one for Grace as well.

And shortly afterwards they packed up and went back to the house where Brett invited the McKinnons to stay for drinks.

They stayed for about an hour and it was so pleasant, Ellie felt more relaxed than she had for days.

But finally Archie stood up and drew Delia to her feet. 'Well, beloved—' he kissed her '—we should go but— do you think we'll be able to tear Grace away?' Grace and Simon were watching television together in the den.

They all laughed and it was arranged that Grace would receive an invitation to the school play.

But although Simon watched the car all the way down the drive, he was reticent on the subject of Grace McKinnon. In fact they were all reticent, Ellie noticed, but as if a peace of sorts had descended on the house after a lovely afternoon—or, more accurately, on herself and Brett. She made macaroni cheese for supper, then she went out to water the garden.

That was where Brett found her, barefoot and enjoying the smell of damp earth.

'I can't get over what you've done for this garden.' He looked around. She was watering the herbs and the air was fragrant with, not only damp earth, but peppermint and rosemary, thyme and dill. 'Enjoy yourself?'

'Yes. They're very nice. Why did Delia only marry Archie three years ago? You said something last week about always thinking they were made for each other. And they do seem to be.'

He pushed his hands into his pockets. 'I guess you don't always see what's right in front of you. Archie was always crazy about Delia but she...I don't know, maybe she wanted to spread her wings. Then she fell for a married man, had Grace, but when it came to the crunch he didn't leave his wife.'

'Nice that it's had a happy ending,' Ellie commented and moved along to the roses.

Brett followed, untangling the hose for her where it had got into a knot. 'It took him at least three years to convince her that he didn't feel sorry for her.' He pulled a large handkerchief from his pocket and wiped his hands.

'He told you that?'

'Yes, he did. Could that be the problem with us, Ellie?'

For a moment the spray of water strayed to the path. 'There's a vast difference between you and Archie McKinnon, Brett,' she said eventually.

'Because he was always in love with Delia? Possibly, but pity doesn't come into it now, with us.'

'Pity must have come into it to start with,' she said and moved to the hibiscus hedge. The hose tangled itself once more.

'Bloody hell,' he muttered as he straightened it and wiped his hands again. 'Would you mind standing still for while, Elvira Madigan?'

'I wish you wouldn't call me that.'

'I told you once before I thought it was a pretty name.'

'It's also a tragic name.'

'Ellie…' he paused and studied her bent head with a frown '…are you feeling tragic?'

She swallowed something in her throat. 'No, of course not.'

'What, then?'

She glanced up at him swiftly, then she said straightly, 'When you see two people in love like that, it's probably quite natural to feel a little discontented, that's all.'

'I see. So you could never imagine feeling that way about me?'

She opened her mouth to say that wasn't the problem, but saw the trap. So she said nothing, and moved on.

Only to have the hose taken out of her hand and the water shut off at the nozzle.

'Brett, I haven't finished.'

'Well, I'm tired of untangling hoses and having this conversation on the run.' He put his hands on her shoulders and turned her to face him with something unusually grim in his expression. Then he sighed and his expression changed to quizzical. 'You're a hard woman to deal with, you know? OK, back to the drawing-board.'

Her lips parted. 'What does that mean?'

'Wait and see.' He released her. 'By the way, Chantal called on the phone this morning while you were asleep.'

'She did? What…about?'

'Apparently, she underestimated Dan Dawson when you and she cooked up the plan to get him off your back.'

'Ah. Oh, well—'

'Exactly what advice did you give him?'

'I…er…told him to be persistent but not too obvious,' Ellie said awkwardly.

Brett grinned.

He moved his palms on her shoulders and bent his head to kiss her very delicately until her lips parted beneath his. Then he drew her closer and his kiss deepened. When they stopped he was breathing heavily and she was trembling like a taut bow line in his arms, her body ready to sing to any tune he liked to call.

'How persistent do I have to be, Ellie?' he asked with a tinge of irony.

Her breath came in a little jolt and colour flooded beneath the clear skin of her cheeks.

But the interrogation wasn't over, she discovered as

he said then, 'You do realize only Simon stands between us going to bed right now?'

It was all too true but brought her no comfort in any sense. Physically it was a form of torture to contemplate going to bed with him and knowing it couldn't happen. Mentally it was a form of torture to even attempt to tell herself, Forget about 'couldn't' happen, 'shouldn't' is the operative word.

And, sensually, she was lost in the heaven of his hard embrace, the roughness of his jaw against her cheek, the wisdom of his lean, strong hands that touched her exactly where she wanted to be touched, needed it desperately, even...

It was sheer hell as he gradually released her.

'But Simon won't always be around.' He touched his fingers gently to her cheek—and walked away.

The next morning, Gemma Arden rang to say that her day wasn't going as planned and could she postpone their lunch? Ellie agreed but it turned out that Monday fortnight was the soonest they could fit together.

It was on Tuesday that Ellie remembered Brett's remark about 'back to the drawing-board' and his advice, when she'd queried it—to wait and see.

On Tuesday evening, she began to see the light...

At dinner of roast pork and all the trimmings, Brett made a series of suggestions. That on Saturday they and the McKinnons go to the movies. A new comedy had hit town and Simon was delighted with the suggestion, although he posed the question of whether the adults would enjoy it.

'You know Archie,' Brett said wryly. 'Sounds right up his street! How about you, Ellie?'

'I would love to see it,' Ellie said simply.

'Done, then. If we go to a matinée, we could have a meal afterwards. Next thing—' he helped himself to some more of the pork crackling she'd crisped to perfection '—I think we should hire a cleaning lady.'

'Oh, I don't mind—' Ellie began.

'I do,' he said firmly. 'You have too many talents to be a good little handmaiden to two messy blokes so I propose someone who comes in twice a week to do the heavy cleaning and the ironing. We won't interfere with your therioptic cookery—that would be like shooting ourselves in the foot,' he said gravely. 'What do you reckon, Simon?'

Simon looked at his mother with new eyes. 'Seconded!' he said crisply.

'And last but not least,' Brett went on, 'I've been offered a dog.'

'*Yes!*' Simon shot up from his chair.

'What kind of a dog and who by?' Ellie enquired.

'One of my staff. They have eight little Blue Heeler puppies to dispose of in about two weeks' time.'

'Uh-h-h!' Simon closed his eyes in sheer bliss. Since a Blue Heeler with black points had been used in a series of motor car ads, Simon had longed for one himself. 'Mum?' He turned to her, his blue eyes pleading.

Ellie hesitated, conscious of Brett's rather narrowed gaze on her as well. *What if we leave?* It ran through her mind. What if we have to move to a unit? Why are you doing this—tying me down like this, Brett Spencer?

'Mum, I swear I'll look after it—hey! They run dog-training classes on the cricket oval every Saturday morning. I bet you I could make it as smart as any dog you know.'

Ellie stared into his blue eyes. In fact, Simon had been dying for a dog for years. She'd refused for the same reason she should be refusing now—just in case they had to move. But was it not another facet of his life? And how could she refuse the one breed of dog Simon would be devastated to miss out on?

She sighed inwardly. If they did move on they'd just have to move to a place that took dogs... 'OK...'

She received a bear-hug of pure joy from her son but Brett said nothing. Was it her imagination, though, or did she see a faint glimmer of satisfaction in his grey eyes? she wondered. He went out shortly after dinner so she was unable to put it to the test or take issue with his methods.

That was Tuesday. On Wednesday evening he arrived home with a desk-top computer and enquired whether either of them would have any use for it.

Simon and Ellie looked at each other.

'Could we ever!' Simon pronounced.

'Simon—'

But her son went on blithely, 'The situation is, Brett, that Mum and I have done a computer course together, and I get to use them at school, she does at work, but so far we haven't been able to afford one of our own. We've got a fund going—hey! Let's make it a joint venture! We'll contribute our fund towards it.'

'Simon,' Ellie said firmly, 'our fund at this stage would contribute to about one twentieth of a computer. And it's very important work Brett does so I'm sure he wouldn't want anyone else on his computer.'

'The situation is, Ms Madigan,' Brett said smoothly, 'when we ordered computers for the laboratory, we overestimated our needs so this one is redundant. On discovering this, I purchased it at a discount thinking that this...household could probably use one. As for my ''very important work'', I will be doing all that on my new laptop.'

'May I have a word with you in private?' Ellie said to Brett.

'Sure,' Simon replied for Brett. 'I was just going to nip over to Martie's anyway. When will dinner be ready, Mum?'

'Dinner?' Ellie looked at him distractedly, as if dinner were in league with flying to the moon. 'Uh—in an hour.'

'OK, I'll be back. That should give you plenty of time to sort this out.' He slung on his baseball cap, backwards, and disappeared through the kitchen door.

'There are times,' Ellie said slowly and with perfect enunciation, 'when…' She paused and looked suddenly stricken.

'You could strangle him?' Brett suggested. 'Don't worry, my mother had the same problem with me.'

'I can believe that!' Ellie replied fervently and looking slightly less stricken. 'Between the two of you, you're enough to drive me insane!'

'What's so bad about bringing home a redundant computer that would only gather dust otherwise?' he asked.

'Couldn't you have returned it and got a refund?'

He shrugged. 'Probably. As a research tool for your profession, though, I thought it would be—helpful.'

Ellie moved a couple of pots around on the stove, not quietly. 'When do I get the time for that?' she asked bitterly.

'Well, that's my other point. Once you have some help in the house, you should have a lot more time for doing the things you enjoy.'

Ellie sighed and turned away from the stove, to study him. 'Brett, you're trying to *buy* me.'

'Why would I want to buy you, Ellie,' he countered with a dangerous glitter in his eyes, 'when I could have you free, gratis and for nothing?'

She flushed brilliantly but soldiered on. 'You're making it impossible for me to tear Simon away, you're using Simon to keep me as a hostage and you're doing it deliberately. You went back to the drawing-board and this is what you came up with! It's *blackmail*. You even d... You even diabolically,' she repeated as her voice got clogged up, 'hit on the one breed of dog Simon adores.'

'There was nothing diabolical about it,' he denied. 'I had no idea he was such a fan of that dog but most boys love dogs, they love the companionship, and you were the one who was trying to round out Simon's life as much as you could, although disastrously to date. No pun on words intended,' he added with irony. 'Or was there? Some of your dates were obviously disasters.'

Ellie literally saw red at this piece of logic—for all that she herself had thought along exactly the same lines, at times. 'If you say one more word about dates—' she gripped the handle of an empty pot '—I'll do something I won't regret!'

He eyed the pot warily, then moved forward and prised her fingers off the handle. 'Ellie, you're over-reacting.'

'I'm not,' she whispered as he towered over her. 'I'm doing everything I can to prevent us making an awful mistake, Brett, that's all.'

'What could possibly be so awful about it?' he asked dryly.

She stared at him.

'Do you object to living with me as we are and have been for the past few weeks?' he persisted.

'No, but—'

'So I don't have any habits that drive you crazy or make your skin crawl?'

Ellie licked her lips. 'No… Well, you do like to get your own way.'

He smiled briefly. 'Is there anything I've done that hasn't benefited both you and Simon?'

'Brett, all right.' She swallowed. 'Most things you say make sense but what happens when you fall out of lust with me? What happens to Simon then?'

'Or—do you mean—what happens to Elvira Madigan then?'

'I can never separate myself from Simon,' she said, wilfully choosing to misunderstand him because she was terrified that he'd seen right through to her heart.

'Who doesn't take that risk, Ellie?' His gaze was intent and probing. 'But is it only lust between us?'

'I've been here for eleven years, Brett.' It came out against her better judgement and she closed her eyes briefly.

'Things change,' he said slowly. 'Then again, others don't. You were fascinating then although I chose not to act on it; you're fascinating now.'

'And in between times?'

'We both got on with our lives. Why don't you just give in, Ellie? Believe me, you'd love it.'

Something flickered in her eyes. 'Simon…'

'There's something else I had in mind for Simon but I'd never do it without consulting you first.'

'What?' she asked. 'Not boarding-school—I'd never agree to that!'

'I'd hardly be suggesting getting him a dog and sending him to boarding-school in the same breath.' He paused and studied her. 'I don't know if you remember but I was the one who packed Tom's things up and settled his affairs?'

She took a breath. 'Yes.'

'I've still got them—his personal things. Some photos, his cricket bat, his golf clubs, his old school tie, the pen he won as a maths prize at school—odds and ends like that. I thought, the next time Simon mentions him, we might, all three of us, go through them together.'

This time Ellie exhaled deeply and there was a suspicious dampness about her eyes.

'Would that be a yea or a nay, Ms Madigan?' he asked softly.

Her shoulders slumped and she looked at the floor.

He put his arms around her and rested his chin on her head. 'There are so many things I admire about you, Ellie. Your spirit and grit, the wonderful home you make, your dedication to your career, the free soul I see in you when you fly your kites.'

He moved her away a little so he could look down into her eyes and disturbed a look of surprise in them. 'You didn't realize I saw it?'

'No.'

'I did. Then,' he went on, his gaze moving lower, 'well, I won't go into details, this being the G-rated hour before dinner, but—well, we both know how—expressive—you can be.' He waited, his gaze firmly fixed on her breasts.

But for once fate, or something, was on her side. She was wearing a dress. Sleeveless, with a square neck, loose, apricot and white gingham with a fine blue stripe added, but not only was it loose, it was made of seersucker cotton, full of little bobbles of fabric, in other words, that made it quite concealing.

When this began to dawn on Brett he raised his eyes

to hers to find the little golden points in her eyes gleaming in a way that told him she had scored against him and not only knew it but was amused by it.

What followed took him even more by surprise, however. She freed herself from his arms and stood gazing at him with her expression rearranged to serious. Then she stepped forward, cupped his face in her hands and murmured, 'Two can play that game, Brett Spencer.'

'Undoubtedly,' he agreed, but found himself suddenly mesmerized by the sheen of her lips, the clean shine and perfume of her hair, the slender line of her throat.

'And this.' She drew her palms down to his chest and moved closer.

Almost of their own accord, his arms circled her and she moved even closer so that the slender lines of her body were imprinted on his—and his immediate reaction was to take an unexpected breath at the involuntary response this drew from him.

She smiled, not in triumph but something wiser and eternally feminine. And she stood on tiptoe and rested her lips against his, but just as he made a move to crush her to him she slipped away from him.

'Ellie,' he said huskily, 'what was that all about?'

She shrugged delicately. 'Something for you to think about, perhaps?'

'Think?' he repeated.

'It's what I get told to do a lot and I'm sure it's good for anyone to shake up their thoughts occasionally.' She looked at him gravely. 'For example, you seem to be so sure of a lot of things in relation to me, Brett, but what do you *really* know about it?'

And she moved serenely into the dining room where she began to set the table.

'What about the computer?' He stood in the doorway watching her.

She looked over her shoulder. 'It can stay so long as there are no more similar gestures.'

'How kind of you, Ellie,' he said harshly.

But not even that dented her composure. She glinted him an enigmatic little look and went on with what she was doing. And Simon came noisily through the back door.

CHAPTER SEVEN

A TRUCE reigned for the next few days.

Brett and Simon consulted on a suitable kennel for the new dog and decided to build one themselves.

The computer was installed and a cleaning lady, recommended by Delia, was acquired. A vigorous woman in her mid-forties who'd come armed with a list of the products she preferred to use. After her first day, Ellie felt jittery and as if her privacy had been invaded despite the gleaming floors and absence of an overflowing ironing basket to make her feel guilty.

'What's wrong?'

Brett stopped on his way out to the garage where the great kennel construction was under way with a lot of banging. He had a saw in one hand and a metal tape measure in the other, having requested leave to borrow them from her kite-making tools.

She was sitting at the kitchen table in a brown study. 'Nothing.'

'You don't seem to be jumping for joy over your clean house,' he observed.

'I am, well, I found it a little hard to handle, that's all.'

He hesitated. 'Perhaps you'd be better away from the house while she's here—is that the problem? Feeling underfoot all the time?'

'That,' Ellie agreed, 'and the fact that she rearranged all the ornaments and I found it hard to…give orders, I suppose.'

'How do you treat a cleaning lady kind of thing?' he hazarded. 'Simple. Be friendly, have a cup of tea with her occasionally, but be quite clear on what you want her to do. Don't leave it all up to her, in other words. That's a sure way to lead to complacency.'

'How do you know all this?' Ellie enquired with a glimmer of humour.

'Handling staff requires a universal technique whether they're lab assistants, interns or cleaning ladies. A friendly but firm touch.' He looked at the tools in his hands and became rueful. 'Building kennels, on the other hand, is not my area of expertise.'

'Why did you agree to it, then?'

A look of frustration crossed his face. 'It's only a box with a roof on it, I thought it would be a piece of cake!'

'Would you like a hand?'

'No. Thank you, but no,' he said with dignity. 'My pride has taken a bit of a hammering as it is so I intend to succeed here.'

'Your...?'

'As you very well know,' he said softly.

Ellie looked away first and he went back to the kennel.

But in the peace of the kitchen she pondered the nature of the truce that reigned at 3 Summerhill Crescent. Had she really given Brett something to think about? If so, what was he thinking? What would be his next step?

His very next step was to hammer a finger instead of the nail he'd been intending to bang into the kennel, with an accompanying yell and a string of curses that nearly took the roof off.

When the tumult had subsided somewhat, i.e. he'd been taken to hospital, had it X-rayed to establish whether he'd broken it—he hadn't but it was severely bruised—and had it bound up securely with all his fingers on that hand immobilized on a splint for pain relief, and they were back home, she said, 'I thought doctors were particularly nimble-fingered?'

He looked at her broodingly over the tea she'd made to revive them all. 'Surgeons are. I'm a different kind of doctor.'

'But surely all doctors learn to operate to a certain level?'

'There's a vast difference between building a kennel and operating on a human being, Ellie!'

'Mum, leave it,' Simon advised. He turned to Brett. 'I wouldn't worry about it, mate,' he said kindly. 'We can't all be good at everything and Martie's dad has all the right tools. He'll finish it off for us. I'm going to bed, I'm worn out. Goodnight.'

'Goodnight,' Ellie and Brett chorused.

'He's right,' Ellie said reasonably. 'We can't all be good at everything.'

'When has your son being right, even if you damn well know it, not produced a sense of ire in you if not to say all the indignity of role reversal?' he enquired acidly.

Ellie hid a smile. 'It can be a bit demoralising, I agree. But—'

'Hell! Don't *you* start humouring me, Ellie!'

She sat back. 'OK. I won't say another word.'

He watched her darkly as she sipped her tea then folded her hands in her lap. 'That doesn't mean to say you have to stop talking to me!'

'What would you like to talk about?'

He regarded his immobilized left hand with huge irritation. 'As a matter of fact I don't want to talk at all. What I would really like is something quite different.'

'Such as?' she asked, unwisely as it happened.

'I'd like someone to take me to bed and make love to me very gently, then hold me in her arms until I fell asleep. I'd like some TLC, in other words.'

For a moment Ellie was truly tempted as they stared into each other's eyes. To be able to kiss away his blues and lead him down a path of delight for both of them would be heaven, she freely acknowledged. To know that he actually needed her... No, don't even think about it, she advised herself.

She stood up. 'Brett, if I were ever to do that, I think you would be much happier to have full use of both hands. But I do have a light sedative they gave me at the hospital in case you had trouble sleeping.'

Several expressions chased through his eyes. 'I told you this once before, but you're a hard woman, Ellie. It's going to take more than a light sedative to get me to sleep now.'

'Don't you believe it. Goodnight,' she said.

He stood up himself. 'Before you go, Ellie.' He slipped his good arm around her waist, pulled her close with surprising strength and said to her look of surprise, 'Just thought I'd give you a demonstration of what I can do one-handed.' He bent his head and started to kiss her in a way that told her plainly he wouldn't take no for an answer.

In fact he kissed her breathless and managed to balance his injured hand lightly on her shoulder at the same time. Then he let her go. 'There. Take that to bed with you, Elvira.'

She licked her bruised lips and put her hands to her heart in an attempt to slow it down while her body was racked with sensual anticipation that was going to go unrequited because, apart from anything else, she was quite sure she hated him at the moment at least. And her eyes were distinctly stormy as she said tautly, 'Talk about a boyish attempt to salvage your pride!'

'Oh, I don't know about that,' he drawled. 'Some pride may have been involved.' His lips twisted. 'But if you can't take the heat with a real man, perhaps you should get out of the kitchen?'

Ellie looked around wildly. They so happened to be in the kitchen.

Which caused him to look briefly amused. 'That was a figure of speech.'

'It had better be,' she said between her teeth and clenched her fists. 'What's more, if you weren't already injured, I'd...'

She stopped as he took one of her hands and uncurled her fingers. And to her great surprise he lifted her hand to his mouth and kissed her fingers. Then, with a rather weary sigh, he said, 'Go to bed, Ellie. This is getting all out of proportion.'

He returned her hand to her and turned away.

She went to bed but not to sleep, for ages, anyway.

First of all, she was still seething about men. Men, who could kiss you against your will and issue insults when their pride got trampled—when had she ever insulted him? she asked herself bitterly. Surely her remark about doctors being nimble-fingered couldn't have dented his ego to that extent? And then, she marvelled, they could accuse you of making mountains out of molehills.

But finally the seething gave way to some inexplicable tears and a tired feeling of confusion—and loneliness. So lonely and muddled and unhappy, in fact, she even got up once and stood beside her door desperate for some kind of relief...

If anyone needs some TLC, she thought ruefully, it's me.

But in the end she didn't have the nerve to do it, and she went sadly back to bed.

'What the hell happened to you?' Archie McKinnon stared at Brett's hand.

'Don't ask,' Brett replied. They'd just met up with the McKinnons outside the cinema complex.

'Could have happened to anyone,' Simon offered.

'Thanks, pal,' Brett said. 'In fact it probably could not, but the least said the better. Shall we?' He gestured for them to enter the cinema foyer.

Causing Delia to cast Ellie a laughing little look of enquiry as they dropped back a bit behind the rest of the party.

Ellie explained briefly, finishing up, 'But don't tell him I told you. He's not in a very good mood.'

'Cross my heart,' Delia promised. 'Men!' she added with so much feeling Ellie had to laugh, and found herself feeling a lot better. A process that had actually begun on seeing Grace in a denim overall dress with a red and white striped T-shirt and her hair in two bunches with red ribbons—and the way Simon's face had lit up at the sight of her.

And, satisfyingly laden down with popcorn and Coke, they all made their way to their seats.

Approximately ninety minutes later they emerged and even Brett was still laughing.

They had a lively dinner at a pavement restaurant and finally took their respective offspring to their respective homes.

'Thank you for that,' Ellie said to Brett. 'I hope it wasn't too…young for you.'

'I enjoyed it and I especially enjoyed seeing Grace and Simon enjoy it so much. You too,' he added rather wryly.

Ellie grimaced. 'There is still, obviously, a bit of a kid in me. How's your finger?'

'Throbbing a bit.'

She hesitated.

He waited, giving her his grave attention.

'Er...nothing,' she said lamely.

He smiled like a tiger at play; lazily, humorously, but never leaving you in doubt that, verbally anyway, he could demolish you.

'I'm going to bed,' Ellie said hastily.

'Why not?' he mused gently. 'We both probably need a good night's sleep.'

Ellie set her lips at the innuendo—that she had spent as uncomfortable a night as he had—and decided to counter it. 'I certainly do.' She shrugged. 'It's my market morning tomorrow so I have to be up at the crack of dawn.' And she strolled away to her bedroom.

She'd always loved a market atmosphere, and to have her own stall amidst the bustle was an extra pleasure.

There were a myriad products for sale: clothes, fresh produce, pot plants, cut flowers, art and craft work, home-made jams, chutneys and preserves, biscuits and cakes—but only one kite stall. And she'd recently acquired a folding canopy so she and her kites were protected from the elements. She also had two folding chairs and a picnic hamper. In fact, during a lull, she was pouring herself a cool drink from a Thermos flask when Chantal strolled past, did a double take, and came back.

'Ellie!'

Ellie looked up, and froze for a moment. 'Hi!' she

said belatedly. And added, because she felt guilty on
several fronts in regard to Chantal Jones, 'Have you got
time for a cold drink?'

'Sure do!' Chantal plonked herself down in the other
chair, removed the picture hat she wore with very short,
tight shorts and a bikini top, and fanned herself with it.
'It gets bloody hot in this part of the world!'

Ellie delved into the basket and produced another
plastic glass. 'Here you go. Very cold, home-made lemonade. Chantal...' she paused and sat down herself '...I
hope you don't hate me?'

Chantal studied her glass, then raised her remarkable
violet eyes. 'I thought about it,' she said slowly, and
Ellie held her breath. Then the other girl giggled suddenly and went on, 'Do you have any idea how persistent Dan Dawson can be?'

Ellie grimaced. 'I'm afraid I told him to be...well, I
actually told him to be persistent but not too obvious,'
she confessed.

'That explains why I'm here—' Chantal looked
around ruefully '—at a market.'

Ellie's eyebrows shot up. 'You're here with Dan? At
his suggestion?'

'Yep! Nice, clean, *not too obvious* fun, I guess.
Although we are going to South Bank for lunch.'

Ellie's lips quivered, although she still looked a bit
mystified. 'But he knows I have a stall here—and where
is he?'

Chantal waved a hand. 'There's a toy-train exhibition
over there. He was entranced so I left him to it—told
him I'd wander around on my own for a bit. And he
obviously doesn't mind the thought of me bumping into
you—men are really weird sometimes.'

Their gazes locked.

'What did Brett tell you about us?' Ellie asked nervously.

Chantal continued to study her. 'He told me he was going to marry you come hell or high water, Ellie,' she said at last.

Ellie's mouth dropped open.

Chantal frowned. 'You didn't know?'

Ellie looked confused. 'I know now—I mean, not the come hell or high water bit, although I've started to suspect it lately—but, for Simon's sake, he's decided it's a good idea.'

'And for your sake?'

Ellie dropped her gaze from the acute little query in Chantal's eyes and sipped some lemonade.

'How long have you been in love with him?'

Chantal's words hung in the air.

'From the day he rescued me beside a parking meter eleven years ago,' Ellie said barely audibly and closed her eyes briefly. 'That is so unbelievable,' she added.

'Why?'

Ellie hesitated. 'I told you about Tom? Well, he'd barely gone from me, it was only a few months so it makes me feel…terrible.'

Chantal sat forward. 'Honey, these things happen.' She grimaced. 'If it's any consolation, I was coming home to get engaged to a guy when I happened to sit next to Brett Spencer on a plane. Next minute,' she said dryly, 'I've forgotten all about that guy.'

Ellie had to smile, although faintly. And she said, 'I know you're trying to help but that makes it worse, not better. I feel as if I've joined a club.'

'Oh, eleven years puts you into a category of your own, Ellie,' Chantal assured her, and paused thoughtfully. 'But, for all that I sometimes go over the top there's one thing I hold very dear.'

Ellie looked at her questioningly.

'In relation to men especially—my self-esteem.'

Ellie glanced up and down the gorgeous length of Chantal Jones. 'You…you have the fire-power to be able to do that,' she suggested.

'Don't you believe it. If I let myself, I could be just as vulnerable as the next girl, if not more so. I don't. If I make a mistake, I pick myself up and start all over again. What I'm trying to say is, don't feel guilty because you fell in love with another man when you thought you shouldn't. If *that's* what's colouring your feelings for Brett, a lack of self-esteem because of *that*, throw it out of the window with the bath water because it happens, is all.'

Ellie opened her mouth to deny the charge but she paused suddenly, and frowned.

'I thought so,' Chantal murmured.

'It's not the only reason,' Ellie said slowly.

'Maybe not but it's a start. What else is there?'

'He…seems so certain he can make me deliriously happy!'

They looked at each other, and started to laugh together.

'All right,' Ellie said, 'maybe he can. I don't know if I can do the same for him.'

'What's that got to do with the price of eggs?' Chantal asked.

Ellie stared at her.

'If you don't, you don't—so you pick yourself up and move on.'

'There's Simon, though.'

'Kids live through it all the time. And correct me if

I'm wrong, but I don't think Brett Spencer is one to fool around lightly with a kid's well-being and happiness.'

'Are you suggesting I marry him?' Ellie asked bluntly.

Chantal waved her hat. 'I did my best—worst, maybe,' she said wryly, 'and now it's time to move on, if that's what you mean.'

'With…Dan, perhaps?'

Chantal shrugged. 'Who knows?' She looked around. 'I guess no one could have dragged me to a market if I wasn't just a touch intrigued.'

Ellie gave a genuine smile.

'But I'll tell you something else, Ellie,' Chantal commented. 'If it's not your money they're after, men marry for a variety of reasons—sex, sex and sex. If you get that right, you're in with a heck of a chance.' She stood up. 'But if there's one thing Brett Spencer taught me—they still like to be the hunters rather than the hunted.'

Ellie stood up herself, laughing. 'I'll remember your words of wisdom. It's been a pleasure knowing you, Chantal—I hope we meet again!'

'Sell many kites today?' Dictt noked when she got home.

He was lazing beside the pool in a pair of colourful board shorts with the Sunday papers spread haphazardly around him and weighted down with stones from the rockery.

'Four. An average day. How's your finger?'

He looked at her gravely. 'Improving. Why don't you have a dip yourself? You look a little hot and bothered.'

'Yeah, I think I will when I've unloaded the car. Where's Simon?'

'He and Martie Webster have gone with Martie's father to watch some trail bike trials up Mount Coot-Tha.

I didn't think you'd mind so I gave my permission on your behalf.'

Ellie pulled a face.

'You do mind?'

'No! I just hope Simon doesn't put in an order for a trail bike, that's all.'

Brett laughed and levered himself off the lounger. 'I'll give you a hand with your stuff. I've never said that literally before.' He looked at his immobilized hand wryly.

'I can manage, don't worry. You relax,' she said and turned away.

'But I do worry, Ellie,' he said slowly. 'You take so much on yourself.'

'Well, I guess I'm used to it,' she replied prosaically, and turned to back to him suddenly. 'You seem to be in a much better mood!'

He looked quizzical. 'That's one of my good points. I may not be all lightness and joy at times but I don't sulk.'

'I'm glad to hear it!' She chuckled.

And, companionably, they unloaded her car. Then she changed into her scarlet one-piece swimsuit, had a dip and came out to find he'd prepared a couple of Margaritas for them.

'This is decadent,' she proclaimed as she dried herself and sank down into a lounger.

'But a nice way to spend a Sunday afternoon?' he suggested.

'Mmm.'

'I was thinking,' he said after a while.

Ellie tensed.

But he surprised her. 'This coming Tuesday is the first Tuesday in November.'

'Melbourne Cup day?'

'The race that stops the nation,' he agreed. 'I have tickets.'

'So?'

'Could you get a few days off?'

She sat up and regarded him askance. 'You mean—go to the Melbourne Cup with you?'

'Ellie—' he grinned '—what's so impossible about that? It's not the moon.'

'It is about a thousand miles away!'

'Two hours by plane—I'm not suggesting we drive or hitchhike or—'

'Why me, Brett?' she broke in firmly and with an 'I'm standing no nonsense' look.

'Why not?'

She floundered for a moment. Then, 'It costs money to fly about the place on a whim!'

'It won't cost you a thing and, before you get your knickers in a *knot*,' he stressed, 'I won't be paying either.'

'How come? I don't understand.' She frowned.

'The company I have some shares in is a sponsor and they're providing it, but I also happen to be a member of the VRC—the Victoria Racing Club.'

'What on earth for? You don't seem to be a racing type—you've hardly been home for so many years!'

'My mother passed it down to me. Her family came from Melbourne. There is actually a house down there that she also passed down to me. At Portsea. On the Mornington Peninsula. It's been leased out for years but the lease has expired and I'd like to have a look at it before I decide whether to sell it or keep it. I also have some other business down there so I could kill several birds with one stone.'

He looked into the distance for a while, then back at her, and remarked gravely, 'I'm so glad you didn't fall back on the ''nothing to wear'' excuse. That's terribly unoriginal.'

Ellie shut her mouth with a click. 'The only reason for that is because I haven't had time to consider that angle. Brett, no, thank you very much, but—'

'We'd be flying down very early on Tuesday morning, Ellie. We'd spend Tuesday night at the Sofitel after the Cup, you'd have your own room. We'd go down to Mornington on Wednesday and you could fly home on Thursday morning—I might have to stay on until Saturday.'

'Apart from anything else,' Ellie said with exaggerated patience, 'I'm just not in a position to go flying off at a moment's notice.'

'The Websters are fine to have Simon. Simon is fine about staying with them and feels the break will do you good.'

'You…*you*…' But she was essentially speechless.

'And, by my reckoning, all the extra work you did while Simon was away at camp should earn you a few days off,' he continued placidly.

Then something sharpened in his grey eyes. 'But, let's be honest. We seem to have reached a stalemate, you and I.' He looked around. 'It may be partly due to this environment. Perhaps things will clarify themselves in a different setting.'

Ellie reached for her Margarita and took a decent sip. Was it a threat? she wondered. Or—it made sense. They couldn't go on the way they were. But what kind of pressure could he exert on her on a trip to the Melbourne Cup? It was—she shook her head—a bizarre suggestion, really.

'You don't think this is an attempt to seduce you, Ellie?' he queried softly.

She gazed at him over the salty rim of her glass and decided to be honest in return. 'It did just occur to me, yes.'

'So I gathered.'

A fleeting smile tugged at her lips. 'You must admit it's an odd way to break a deadlock.'

'Difficult circumstances often require unusual solutions.' He looked at her steadily. 'Or would you really prefer to slug it out here?'

She shivered suddenly and not because she was cold. 'Brett, if I say no after we've taken a rather pointless jaunt to the Melbourne Cup, will you accept it?'

'Yes. But it won't be pointless, Ellie, believe me.'

Simon sat on the end of her bed the next evening while she packed, and offered helpful suggestions.

'What are you going to do about a hat?' he asked. 'You can't go to the Melbourne Cup without a hat. It's unheard of.'

'It probably isn't, you know.'

'Still, you are my mum so it's only natural for me to want you to look your best.' He gazed at her seriously.

'Then just to put your mind at rest, kid—da-da!' She pulled the lid off a box that had been sitting unnoticed on a chair, exposing a supremely chic pale green hat with a wide wavy brim and a green and white silk trim gathered around the base of the crown and tied in a stylish bow at the back.

'Wow!' Simon's eyes widened.

'There's more,' Ellie warned, and she reached into her wardrobe to produce a slim linen dress that exactly matched the hat and a very elegant pair of white high-heeled sandals.

Simon clapped his hands and asked her to model the outfit for him. She did so, taking care to position the hat carefully.

'There.' She turned back from the mirror and stood regally in the middle of the room. 'A mum to be proud of, you reckon?'

Simon jumped off the bed. 'You bet!' He hugged her carefully. 'I'm sure Brett will be proud of you too.'

Ellie grimaced and took the hat off. 'That's the computer fund and a little bit of the kite fund gone—oh, well.'

'It's all in a good cause,' Simon assured her.

She hesitated. 'What do you mean?'

'You need a break and a bit of fun! Now don't worry about me, I'll be fine at Martie's—we're going to work on the kennel with Martie's dad. Martie is green with envy, by the way!'

Ellie smiled a bit mechanically but Simon didn't notice.

And she tossed and turned a bit before she fell asleep later that evening because it all seemed to come back to one thing—how was she ever going to tear Simon away?

But a vision of Chantal swam into her mind—and her advice ran through Ellie's mind. She grinned to herself as she remembered the more outrageous bits of it. Then she sat up suddenly at the question of self-esteem Chantal had raised. Did she lack self-esteem with regard to Brett? Was that as much the core of her problem as anything else?

She lay back and thought dryly that circumstance had had a lot to do with that, but she'd always been aware of it. How much had her perceived defection from Tom to Brett Spencer poisoned her confidence in herself as a woman, though, she wondered, and her ability to make choices? She certainly didn't have a good record in that line.

Then it occurred to her that perhaps the one lesson she could learn from Chantal was, if a man let you down, you picked yourself up and moved on. And she fell asleep thinking of going to the Melbourne Cup...

Since they were going straight to Flemington racecourse by helicopter from Tullamarie airport, Ellie dressed for the races before she left home, although she carried her hat. She also carried a raincoat because the Melbourne weather was notoriously fickle and renowned for producing all four seasons in one day.

But it was a beautiful day as they stepped onto the hallowed turf of Flemington, the roses were glorious, the crowd already huge and the buzz of excitement in the air was incredible—and infectious. Ellie started to feel excited herself and very pleased she'd splurged on a new outfit and hat as they were ushered into the members' stand.

Not only on her own account was she pleased—Brett was looking particularly distinguished in a blue suit, a crisp white cotton shirt and the club tie. His bruised finger was the only finger now bandaged and encased in a leather finger-guard. He had also commented flatteringly on her outfit. And he was an attentive companion. But something else came home to Ellie during the afternoon. He'd always played his background down and, while she knew it was wealthy, she hadn't realized the extent of it or how influential it was.

Now, she couldn't doubt it as many obviously wealthy and influential people greeted him delightedly, people who hadn't seen him for five years but remembered him well.

However, all of these impressions sank beneath the sheer excitement of the races; the august privileges of being in the members' stand such as being able to get into the mounting yard to watch the horses parade; to actually touch and smell the roses that lined it and the corridor that led to the track. And she partook of a champagne lunch as the tension in the air grew and finally it was time for the big race.

She made her selection, backed the horse she liked and they climbed up into the stand to watch the pre-Melbourne Cup festivities. Against the background of the city of Melbourne, there were skydivers who landed on the track, there was a pipe band that paraded up and down the track; there were the weird hats and outfits amongst the huge—over a hundred thousand people— hugely good-humoured crowd. And finally, the horses.

'Oh, I'm so excited!' She bounced up and down in her chair. 'What have you backed?'

He looked at her wryly. 'I've never seen you like this, Ellie. Uh—' He told her which horse he'd backed.

'Very wise,' she commented.

'You know something I don't?'

'Not a thing!'

'So?'

'I backed it too, for the princely sum of five dollars— because I like the name.' She bestowed a beatific smile on him. 'Brett,' she said on a sudden thought, 'talking horses, are you going to get back into polo?'

His expression changed rather drastically for a moment, then he said simply, 'No.'

She raised an eyebrow at him.

'I don't have the time, Ellie. Look, they're starting to

load the horses into the barrier. Our horse is being a bit fractious.'

'Oh, no!' Her attention flew back to the track and she took the binoculars he offered her. Then she breathed a sigh of relief as their horse consented to be led into his stall. 'He's in!' She handed the binoculars back and gripped her hands tightly in her lap.

Minutes later the red light blinked on top of the barrier stalls, indicating that the field was under starter's orders, and moments later, to an enormous roar from the crowd, the gates flew open and the race was under way.

Approximately three minutes and twenty seconds later, Ellie leapt up and tossed her hat into the air—a winner!

Brett caught the hat and took her in his arms.

'How clever was that?' she enthused, her eyes shining.

'Not only clever but gorgeous as well, Ms Madigan,' he said, and kissed her soundly.

And a mysterious change seemed to creep into how things were between them from that moment on; a subtle closeness developed so that they were no longer two people enjoying the Melbourne Cup together, but two people enjoying each other.

After watching the presentation, he took her down and out into the public areas to enjoy the crowd but kept her hand in his as they laughed at the novelties they saw and the antics of the crowd. They found a stall that sold Cup memorabilia and bought Simon a cap, then one for Martie Webster as well.

And when they got in a crowd jam, he put his arms around her and she took her hat off and rested her cheek below his shoulder, feeling safe and secure while they waited for it to clear. And at the end of the day, there was a limousine to take them to their hotel.

*   *   *

They had a two-bedroomed suite in the soaring tower at the Sofitel on Collins Street.

Ellie looked round at the elegantly beautiful luxury of it all and turned to Brett. 'Thank you so much for a wonderful day. I had no idea I was going to enjoy it so much.'

He shed his jacket and pulled off his tie. 'It's not over yet.'

She looked a little blank.

'I thought we'd have dinner here in the hotel. Then, if you felt like it, a little flutter at the casino. But there's no rush. You could have a rest.'

Ellie stared at him. 'I don't…know what I feel like doing.'

He came over to her but didn't touch her. And the mysterious current that had flowed between them since he'd kissed her at the races grew stronger.

She frowned and tried to analyze it. Desire—yes. But different from other times. There was more warmth to it in an emotional sense; there was the sheer pleasure of his company and the thought that he'd organised a wonderful day for her.

There was an irresistible urge to let down her guard completely and tell him that, for her, there was only one fitting way to go now—into his arms and his bed.

'Ellie?' he said very quietly.

'Oh, Brett,' she whispered, and against all odds found herself smiling at him because he was in so many ways all that she wanted. She brought her hands up and placed them on his chest. 'I don't want to rest.'

He looked down into her eyes with a gleam of a question in his.

'I want,' she said slowly, 'to be brought to life again. I don't want to make any decisions but I really…need to end this special day in a special way, with you.' She stood on her toes and kissed him lingeringly.

'Ellie.' He hesitated and put his hands on her waist. 'Just promise me one thing—no regrets.'

'No regrets, Brett,' she vowed.

'Because I can think of no better way to end this day either—it's been on my mind for the last few hours.'

'Really?'

'Really. Since you threw your hat in the air, as a matter of fact.'

'Why would that do it?' she asked in a fascinated sort of way.

'Why would that do it?' he repeated. 'It was an expression of pure joy over so much more than winning the princely sum of twenty dollars. It was…' he paused '…a delight to see you being—just you. Not a mother or a housewife or a girl juggling two jobs.'

'That's how I feel—liberated,' she said with a sigh of pleasure.

He kissed the corner of her mouth and his hands moved on her. 'Let's see if we can further that process.' He wound his arms around her and began to kiss her in earnest.

And when she was dizzy with delight, he slipped the zip of her dress down and helped her to step out of it, to reveal her new underwear, worn only once before, to Delia and Archie's anniversary.

'This is very sexy, Ellie,' he said, running his hands down her sides. 'Just as well I didn't know about it earlier, I could have been a basket case.' He looked ruefully into her eyes.

'I like the thought of that!'

'I always knew you were a hard woman.'

'I feel anything but at the moment,' she responded,

and gasped as he slid her briefs down and his fingers explored the curls at the base of her stomach.

'Tell me.'

She tilted her head back and closed her eyes as she was racked by delicious tremors. 'On fire…'

She felt him take an unexpected breath, then he was kissing her throat and the valley between her breasts and all the while exploring her more and more intimately. Then he picked her up and carried her into a bedroom.

She made a little murmur of distress as he placed her on the bed and left her.

'I'll be right back, Ellie.' He dropped a kiss on her hair—and was as good as his word but this time strong, lean, hard and naked.

And he immediately gathered her into his arms and he talked to her while he stroked her—nothing serious, but odds and ends to do with their day—until the magic started to build again. Then she helped him to take her bra off and dispense with her briefs completely, and, if he'd assaulted her senses before, she was helpless and humming with desire and delight like a bird on wire beneath this new assault.

In fact she thought she couldn't bear any more and told him so.

'Yes, you can.' He kissed her all the way down to her navel.

'Brett…' She clutched his arms urgently.

He raised his grey eyes to hers. 'Ellie, if it's been a while we need to take certain precautions.'

'It feels as if it's been all my life! What kind of precautions?'

'The last thing I want to do is hurt you so I need to make sure you're really ready.' And he started at the top again, kissing her that was, but this time he didn't stop at her navel.

'Brett, Brett,' she pleaded as she ran her fingers through his hair, 'I've never been more ready in my life...'

He lifted his head and glinted her a wicked little smile. 'Thank heavens, this is sheer torture!'

But still he was circumspect and her heart beat heavily with gratitude—then the moment came and everything else fled from her mind as she surrendered to incredible joy.

CHAPTER EIGHT

'WHAT would you like to do now?'

Ellie opened her eyes to find Brett staring down at her with his head propped on his elbow and his hand lying proprietorially on her waist.

'Now?' she said dreamily. 'Well. Dinner here, a flutter at the casino, perhaps a stroll along the Yarra—how does that sound?'

'Far too energetic for a man in my position.'

'What's that? Your position?'

He thought for a bit and said very seriously, 'Bewitched, bothered and bewildered—and the owner of a bruised thumb.'

'Oh!' Ellie sat up and picked up his hand. 'Did I hurt it? I'm so sorry.' She kissed his palm gently, then placed it over her breast with her nipple nestled into it.

He groaned.

'Surely that's not hurting?' she said innocently.

'Maybe not, but it could be classified as imposing a severe trial on me,' he returned.

She raised her eyebrows.

'In light of your determination to dine, gamble and walk,' he supplied ruefully.

'I see. Still, if your finger is hurting, those things would be much better for it than—any other activities you might have had in mind,' she said gravely.

He scanned her figure, so slim and pretty, so silky. His gaze lingered on some faint marks on her skin that he himself had made during his possession of her, and finally their gazes locked.

'That's—increasingly—becoming not an option,' he said.

'Ah! Oh, yes, I see! Well, you put your hand out of harm's way,' she suggested, 'and I might be able to come up with a plan.'

Several minutes later, he said, 'Has it occurred to you I could die of this plan?'

Ellie moved cautiously. She was lying on top of him and she said, with the golden glints in her eyes teasing him, 'It's not having that effect on me!'

'How about this?' He caressed her bottom with his good hand.

She took a breath. 'Now that—is rather remarkable but I'm still not dying.'

He made a rough little sound in his throat and, regardless of his sore finger, clamped her hips to his, and together they shot to sheer ecstasy.

'Wow!' Ellie breathed when she could speak again. 'You've wrecked me.'

He stroked her damp curls off her forehead and kissed her lightly.

'It was either that or, well, I told you at the time.'

She snuggled up against him. 'I'm not complaining. In fact being wrecked by you is rather unique.'

'Thank you, Ms Madigan. So. Should we consider our options again?'

'All right. Maybe we should forgo the walk along the Yarra?'

'Good thinking. And the casino might just be a bit lively for us, don't you agree?'

'Definitely. As for getting dressed and going to dinner, even in the hotel—'

'Not a good idea at all,' he broke in.

'Well, we need not make a very long meal of it.'

'The thing is, I have this aversion to you being dressed at the moment,' he said, trailing his fingers down her body. 'And while I'm quite sure you'd create a sensation undressed, I don't think I'd like that at all!'

'Heaven forbid, Mr Spencer!' But her eyes were full of laughter. 'How about room service?'

'Done! You know…' he sobered a little '…you soared like one of your kites, and took me with you, just now. What were you thinking?'

She trailed her fingers down his arm. 'Just that—it was like soaring up to heaven. I didn't know I was capable of…' She stopped.

'Taking a man to heaven with you?'

'Not really, no.' She looked into his eyes with a faint frown.

'I think you should bear it in mind.' He dropped a kiss on her head and went to order room service.

When he came back she was showering.

He stepped in to join her. 'Good thinking—unless you've changed your mind about going out?'

'Far from it. But I do have an outfit that's perfect for…uh…this kind of thing.'

'What exactly is this kind of thing?' He soaped himself vigorously.

'Dining at home—that kind of thing.' She raised her arms and the water streamed all over her from head to toe.

'Damn,' Brett said and took her wrists in one hand.

'Damn?' She tilted her head back so as not to have water in her eyes.

He looked up and down her body. 'I've never seen a

lovelier waterfall, that's all.' He released her wrists and stepped under the jet himself. 'You're like a perfect sprite.'

She touched the smooth, sleek muscles in his upper arms. 'You're amazingly well put together for a doctor.'

'How should doctors be put together?' he enquired gravely.

She grimaced. 'I don't know but it's not very physical work, is it? Whereas you're…very physical.'

He turned the water off, picked her up and took her out of the shower, where he wrapped her in a towel and slung one round his waist.

'Enough of that, my lovely sprite. It was getting dangerous.'

She raised her eyebrows.

'Three times in as many hours,' he elucidated. 'I don't want to wear you out.'

'Thank you for your concern.' She stood on tiptoe and planted a butterfly kiss on his mouth. 'But I just wanted to say something. I may have impugned your…lack of co-ordination when it came to building kennels?' She looked a question at him.

'You did,' he agreed. 'You gave me to understand that in your estimation I was not only downright unhandy as a kennel builder but also a doctor.'

'I take it back—well, kennels may not be your forte but in certain other respects you're…absolutely brilliant!'

He looked down at her wryly, then his eyes softened. 'If you mean what I think you mean, I had the finest material to work with. You.'

She felt a sudden lump in her throat, and sniffed— and there was a knock at the door just as he was about to put his arms around her.

He dropped them. 'Dinner has arrived,' he said, looking wicked, 'at a very fortuitous moment.'

'Danger time again?'

'Uh-huh.' He pushed some tendrils of hair behind her ears and studied her luminous hazel eyes. 'Why don't I go and organise that while you—didn't you say you had something to wear?'

'Yes! Off you go, we'll eat in the lounge. I'll join you shortly.'

'Yes, ma'am,' he said meekly and cast away the towel to stride through to the bedroom and rummage in his bag for a pair of shorts. 'Just don't be too long about it,' he added over his shoulder. 'I could get lonely.' He pulled the shorts on and walked into the lounge, closing the door behind him.

Ellie stared at it for a moment, then she too discarded her towel and waltzed into the bedroom—literally waltzed. She came to rest in front of the dressing-table mirror with her arms extended and her feet crossed and could never remember feeling better or happier in her life. In fact she took a bow to her reflection and smiled at herself. Then she opened her bag and took out the lovely silvery-grey negligée and nightgown she'd so inexplicably purchased when she'd been shopping for something to wear to Delia's party.

The nightgown had a square neck, no sleeves and the neckline was heavily encrusted with ice-coloured lace. The negligée had the same neckline, sleeves and did up at the front via tiny pearl buttons. They were both mid-calf length and when she twirled they fanned out in a beautiful bell. But before she put them on she dried her hair to get most of the moisture out of it, then ran her fingers through it, which was all she had to do—one of the consolations of curly hair. And she smoothed moisturizer all over her body.

Finally, she presented herself in the lounge, but paused on the threshold and looked down at herself. Even two layers of gossamer silk were not exactly concealing.

Brett was twisting the wire off the cork of a bottle of champagne and he said, simply, 'Wow!'

She looked at him with a touch of anxiety in her eyes. 'I've never worn one of these before.'

He put the bottle down. 'Never?'

'No. I've been strictly a pyjama or a cotton nightshirt girl up to now.'

He came over to her and stood looking down at her enigmatically. 'What wrought the change?'

'On your suggestion I went to buy a new outfit for Delia's party and—went a little crazy,' she said in a rather puzzled sort of way.

'A sort of consumer conniption?' he suggested.

She hesitated.

'Or—you had this in mind?' he said softly and took her chin in his hand.

'Possibly,' she whispered. 'But you don't think it's too…?' Words failed her.

He looked down her body. 'I think it's gorgeous, and perfect to dine in.'

'Only in these circumstances, of course!'

'Of course,' he agreed, and put his arm through hers. 'Well, now we've established that you're dressed right for the occasion, may I show you to your seat, ma'am?'

Ellie laughed and relaxed. 'Please do, sir! And if that is champagne, it's exactly what I need!' she said grandly.

He laughed and kissed the top of her head.

They ate oysters, rolled roast pork stuffed with apricots, prunes and rice and a pear galette with ice cream for dessert.

'Fantastic food,' Ellie pronounced as she spooned up the last of her galette.

'Coming from you that is a compliment.'

'Mind you,' she said ruefully, 'by rights we should go for a run around the block.'

'I've got a better idea.' He got up and poured their coffee and topped up their champagne, and set it on the coffee-table in front of the settee. 'Let's relax and watch the ten o'clock news. We may even see ourselves.' He flicked on the television and invited her to sit down next to him.

And they watched the highlights of the Melbourne Cup with much enjoyment although they didn't see themselves.

'What a day!' Ellie laid her head on his shoulder, then she sat up abruptly. 'I didn't ring Simon...'

He pulled her back. 'It'll be OK. Do it tomorrow morning.' He flicked the remote and the television went dark.

She snuggled against him. 'Tell me about Africa, Brett.'

He laid his head back. 'It's rather like a mistress—of the worst kind. Capricious, wilful, then more beautiful than you'd believe so that just when you're convinced it's driven you crazy and frustrated the life out of you, it gets you in again. My last clinic got burnt down twice, once from natural causes, a direct lightning strike, and once from human error—someone watered a pot plant and didn't notice, or even think about it for that matter, that they were also watering a live multiple adapter board. It had four plug placements on it but only two were in use. Electricity is still a novelty in some of the really remote areas.'

'What got you "in again" that time?'

He grinned and nuzzled the top of her head. 'How everyone in the village from grandmothers down turned up to help rebuild the place.'

'That's lovely,' she said. Then she frowned. 'What is their biggest problem? Ebola?'

He sighed. 'The biggest killer in Africa these days is AIDS. Then there's malaria, my speciality and still a huge problem.'

'Still?'

'Still and all.'

'Is that why Ross River Fever interests you? Because it's also mosquito-borne like malaria?'

'It's my speciality, if you like.'

Ellie was quiet for a time. Quiet and drowsy but listening as he went on to talk about Africa and his times there. And a question mark began to hover on the edge of her mind. Or, she thought, the conviction that he would go back one day and the question mark was to do with herself...

But she didn't have the energy to ask herself anything—and she fell asleep in his arms.

Brett raised his head and looked down at her. She was sleeping absolutely peacefully. Not so surprising, he reflected. She'd packed an awful lot into one day. I'd like to see her come up with a good reason for not marrying me now, he thought with a faint smile, and paused.

Talking about Africa had opened all the old magic up for him, but there was a subtle difference, one that he couldn't quite put his finger on. Then he yawned and got up to take his sleeping, silken burden to bed.

* * *

Ellie woke the next morning to the aroma of freshly ground coffee on the air. She sat up and pushed her hands though her hair, looked at her bedside clock but it wasn't there—she wasn't even in her own bed.

Of course! It all came back to her and she lay back with her lips parted in, if not horror, absolute astoundment—a favourite word of Simon's. Brett came in from the lounge at that moment and put a cup of tea down on the bedside table.

'Good morning! You look…astonished.'

He was dressed in jeans and a navy shirt, shaved, brushed and immensely good-looking.

Ellie closed her mouth and sat up again. 'I…am. This…is tea?' She pointed to the cup.

'It is. I thought you were useless without a cup of tea to get you going.'

'I am. Thank you!'

He sat down on the side of the bed. 'So what's so astonishing about me bringing you a cup of tea, Ellie?'

She gazed at him over the rim of the cup she'd picked up. 'I…I smelt coffee, that's all.'

'There is also coffee out there, and breakfast, and there's a hire car waiting for us. I still don't understand the amount of astonishment tea over coffee produced,' he said lightly, but with a wicked little glint in his eye.

She brooded for a moment, then put the cup down and said carefully, 'It wasn't altogether that. I woke up thinking I was at home.'

He looked around. 'So this came as a bit of a shock?'

She followed his gaze. 'This and everything else I did yesterday,' she confessed, and bravely met his gaze.

He picked up her hand and kissed her knuckles. 'You promised me one thing—no regrets.'

'Oh, I don't have *any* regrets!' She broke off and

coloured at the enthusiasm in her voice. 'I just thought you might be a bit surprised, that's all.'

'Ellie…' But he was laughing at her and it was a while before he could speak again so instead he lay down beside her.

'I feel an awful fool,' she said against the cotton of his shirt. 'Uh…things just came out wrong.'

'I hope not.' He cradled her against him. 'Because it sounded to me like a very genuine endorsement of what happened yesterday, and it sounded pretty good to me!'

She relaxed.

'Unfortunately, I know it's early,' he said a few minutes later, very pleasurable minutes, 'but I need to get this show on the road. I'm meeting someone at the house, it's nearly a two-hour drive, and if we don't leave soon we'll be late.'

Ellie sat up. 'How long have I got?'

He glanced at his watch. 'Half an hour.'

'You'd be amazed at what I can do in half an hour, Brett!'

'I wouldn't be at all amazed—I've seen you at work, on me, that is.'

She turned to look at him over her shoulder with the golden glints in her eyes most noticeable. 'Don't tempt me,' she warned.

He sat up swiftly. 'So—you did mean that rather than how fast you can dress, pack and breakfast?' he challenged.

She pretended to consider. Then she said with an elegant little shrug, 'On second thoughts, I'd rather take my time the next time I do it—incidentally,' she added, 'you were the one who…rushed us the last time.'

'For my sins—I was dying, thanks to you.'

She put her hand over his. 'I presume we're staying somewhere where we can be together tonight?'

'We are.'

'There you go, then.'

'Ellie—this is a phone.' He pointed to the bedside table.

'I know that, Brett,' she said, her eyes serenely innocent.

'Well, all I have to do is lift it and make a couple of cancellation calls—and we would have all the time in the world!'

She gazed at him, then touched the back of her hand to his cheek as her mouth curved into a smile. 'Actually, you got it right. What I meant was—I've had years of experience in getting dressed, et cetera, in no time at all!'

For a moment his expression defied description, then he said, 'Hell, I knew that but I don't think it's much good to me now.'

'I'd better remove myself,' she suggested, and slipped out of the bed. 'Besides which, since this is a phone, I need to ring my only son.'

She picked up the phone and Brett lay back with his hands behind his head, looking wry. 'It's just as well I'm such a good-natured guy otherwise I could be rather annoyed. As you have said to me from time to time.'

Ellie dialled the Websters' number, conferred briefly with Martie's mother, then Simon came on. 'How's it going, mon?' he asked cheerfully.

'I'm having a wonderful time, Simon! How's it with you?'

He told her in detail, then asked if he could speak to Brett. Ellie said goodbye and handed the phone over, and, seeing that ten minutes of her half-hour had elapsed, dashed into the shower.

Brett was eating breakfast when she emerged from the bedroom wearing white cotton trousers and a blue and white checked blouse and carrying her bag. 'There—five minutes to spare,' she said triumphantly. '*Are* you rather annoyed?'

He gestured for her to sit down, removed the cover from a plate of bacon and scrambled eggs and poured her coffee. 'I'm rolling with the punches,' he advised her. 'Your only son's as well.'

'What would they be?'

'The kennel has been perfected. He's even chosen a name for the dog and they've painted it above the entrance.'

Ellie grimaced. 'Sorry—but I did point out to you an area where you had considerable expertise. What's he going to call the dog?'

Brett eyed her lazily. 'Guess.'

'Uh—I have no idea.'

'What's his other passion?'

'Cricket?' Ellie said incredulously.

'No, but close—Flipper.'

'I should have known that!' They laughed together and presently left the hotel together to drive down to Portsea.

It was another lovely day and a pleasure to be driving down the Mornington Peninsula. Names she'd heard of often rolled past. Frankston, Mount Eliza, Mount Martha and Port Phillip Bay.

But the house Brett had mentioned rather casually at Portsea was a real eye-opener. Old, solid and white behind impressive gates, it had its own beach and beautiful grounds. In fact both Portsea and its neighbouring suburb of Sorrento shouted one thing to her—old money.

There was a real estate agent to greet them at the house and as he showed them around all sorts of questions bubbled up in Ellie—had Brett ever lived here? Why would anyone sell it unless they had to?

But she asked none of them as she followed in their wake and tried not to look too dazzled.

Finally the inspection was over and they got back into the car. 'So—we're not spending the night here?' she queried as she did up her seat belt.

'No. Down the road a bit. What do you think of it?'

Ellie looked back at the house. 'I think it's wonderful but...' she paused '...I seem to sense—I don't know, something not quite right?'

He shrugged. 'It came down on my mother's side of the family. And it was always the cause—one of the many causes,' he amended, 'of bitter disagreement between my parents. Look, Ellie, I need to go back to the office with the estate agent. Would you like to browse around Portsea for a bit? It's not exactly huge but it's pleasant.'

'Sure.'

So he dropped her off and arranged where to pick her up in an hour. She window-shopped for a while, then sat down to have a long cool drink. And it came to her that she'd learnt quite a bit about Brett over the last twenty-four hours—and not only how much she loved being made love to by him.

There was the Africa bit, as she remembered how he'd spoken of it last night—with true, deep affection, she thought with a little pang. And now there was the revelation that his parents had not got on and a house that brought back unhappy memories. How much had that shaped the man he now was? she wondered. How much bearing did both those things have on the decision that was looming in front of her? A decision she had thrust out of her mind yesterday...

'Penny for them?'

She looked up with a start to see Brett standing beside her. 'Oh, this and that.'

He paused and looked at her narrowly, 'I think I may have been away too long,' he said and held out his hand.

She put hers into it and stood up. 'Not really.' But even to her ears she sounded a bit uncertain.

He smiled into her eyes, causing her to go a little weak at the knees. 'Only a few minutes away, and we'll be in paradise.'

'Paradise?'

'You'll see. Come.' He led her to the car.

A few minutes later she did see. Almost at the end of the peninsula, before it gave way to national park, was Peppers, Delgany, a private home resembling a castle that had been taken over by the Peppers chain and converted to a luxury hotel. And once again Ellie was almost bowled over by, this time, the exquisite taste and wonderful aura of this large country-house-style hotel.

'It's wonderful,' she said as she looked around their suite that overlooked a golf course.

'So are you—but I'm glad you like it.' Brett took her in his arms and kissed her leisurely. 'Tired?'

She leant against him gratefully. 'A bit.'

'It's only to be expected. Here's what I propose. A rest, maybe a long soak in the tub, then I'll take you out to dinner—not here, unfortunately, I neglected to book and the restaurant's full. But the Portsea Hotel is also very nice.'

'Anywhere,' she said, and looked longingly through to the king-size bed.

He laughed. 'Go to it, Ms Madigan.'

'What about you?'

'I've got a few calls to make, I'll do it in here so as not to disturb you.'

'I feel…like a wimp.'

'No, you're not. Will you just do as you're told, Ellie?'

'Yes, sir!'

He woke her an hour and a half later with a kiss and a cocktail, a *crème de menthe frappé*, and the news that he'd run the bath for her.

Ellie sat up and made a small, heartfelt sound in her throat, indicative of feeling quite lousy.

He looked amused. 'Take this into the bathroom with you.' He put the glass in her hand. 'Sip it gently while the bubbles do their work and I guarantee you'll get out feeling a million dollars. There's also a nice view from the bathroom.'

'Bubbles?'

'Have a look.'

She followed him into the bathroom and the bath was full of bubbles towering above the rim. 'I could get lost in there,' she observed, then, on an impulse, turned to him and kissed him. 'You're so sweet,' she told him.

He looked down at her ironically. 'Sweet?'

'Well, sweet, stunning, sensational and very sexy.'

'Thank you—as an ego massager that was first class!'

She grinned at him and recommended he take himself off while she restored herself to full vitality.

The Portsea Hotel had a venerable façade but had been modernized inside. And decks had been added so you could sit outside and look over the bay. There was also a lively crowd in attendance. Brett found them a table on the deck and went to the bistro to order for them.

Ellie looked out over Port Phillip Bay as a blue dusk drew in and acknowledged that Brett's remedies had restored her. She felt relaxed and peaceful. She'd put on blue jeans and the top of the outfit she'd worn to Delia's party, so she also felt trendy and in tune with the rather yuppie crowd.

He came back with a bottle of wine in a cooler, a number and the news that their dinner would be ready in about twenty minutes.

'Do you know this part of the world well, Brett?' she asked as he poured the wine.

'I used to spend holidays down here as a kid, with my grandparents. They owned the house. When they died, they left it to my mother and she leased it out.'

'Why did it cause dissension between your parents?'

He sat back and shrugged. 'My grandparents always felt that my mother married beneath her—and not even a Victorian but a brash Queenslander. You may not realize it but—'

'I had,' she broke in. 'Very old money in this part of the world.'

'Exactly.' He smiled faintly. 'Naturally, my father objected to that. And any evidence of her wealth was anathema to him. It also spurred him on to succeed so that he could provide her with as much as her parents had. The long hard road of that took its toll, unfortunately, and there was often a state of war in their relationship.'

Ellie twirled her glass and frowned.

'I know what you're thinking,' he said. 'I wondered

it often enough myself—those things were only periph-
eral, or should have been, so were they just ill-suited
from the start? Were they two people always destined to
have a love-hate relationship? To this day, I don't
know.'

'Actually, I was wondering how it affected you,' Ellie
said.

He moved restlessly. 'Some of it rubs off, obviously.
So. We both suffered a bit at the hands of our parents.
Here's to us, then. Survivors.' He raised his glass and
she did the same. 'Although, you're the ultimate survivor, Ellie.'

'No.' She put her glass down. 'No better or worse
than the next,' she said tranquilly.

He opened his mouth but their number was called and
the delicious meal he brought back steered them towards
brighter topics of conversation.

'Ellie?'

They were lying together in a pool of light from the
bedside lamp, naked and exploring each other intimately.

'Yes?'

'You're very lovely.' He swept his hands down her
flank. 'Soft and delicate but with an inner core of fire
and strength—it's a fascinating combination.'

'Thanks. I guess it would be fair to say I find you
fascinating.'

'What you're doing right now is extremely—fascinating.'

She raised her head and smiled into his eyes.

He smoothed her hair. 'Home tomorrow. For you,
anyway.'

She tensed slightly. 'Are you staying?'

'For a day or two, that's all. I really want to tie up

all my loose business ends so I don't have to keep coming south once the lab is fully functioning.' He moved and rested his head on his elbow so he could look down at her. 'Is that a problem?' He toyed with her nipples.

'No. I can take myself home.'

'So why did you react to the thought of going home?'

'Only because,' she said with an effort, 'I've been living minute to minute for the last two days.'

'No decisions yet?' he said with a wryly raised eyebrow.

'No. Well, one—if you don't stop doing that shortly I'll…have a conniption on my own.'

'Like hell you will,' he said, and eased himself on top of her. 'See?' he teased. 'We're in this together whether you like it or not.'

'I didn't say that…' But she didn't say any more either as he gradually upped the tempo between them until they were moving rhythmically then more and more urgently, on the brink of that lovely sensation—then it was there and she arched her body beneath his and cried out huskily in sheer joy.

Nor did there seem to be much to say afterwards because it was as if what had happened between them had said it all, and he wrapped her loosely in his arms until they fell asleep.

The Melbourne weather did an about-turn the next morning and they drove back to town through mist and rain.

'I can't believe it, it's freezing!' Ellie said.

'It might be as hot as hell at home.'

'At least you know where you are at home.'

'True.'

'Brett, have you made a decision about the house?' she asked.

'No.' He put the windscreen wipers up a notch and swore beneath his breath as the rain pelted down. 'It's a real dilemma. One part of me says get rid of it, it has unhappy associations, another says it is part of my heritage. But there is a buyer on the horizon. What would you do, Ellie?'

She blinked at him. 'It's got nothing to do—'

He stopped her rather abruptly. 'It could.'

She looked out of her window. 'I still can't answer for me in any way, Brett. But if you're undecided, if I were you, I'd keep it.'

'When will you be able to answer for yourself, Ellie?'

She hesitated briefly then put her hand over his. 'I'm very close to being there, Brett. Would you…could you understand that…difficult times make you very wary, though?'

His grey gaze rested on her and he looked as if he was about to say something impatient, then his eyes softened and he sighed. 'Yes. All right. But I may not be home until Saturday so don't get any strange ideas in the meantime.'

'Such as?' Her lips quivered.

'I don't know! But it might be an idea to talk it over with your only son.'

'My only son,' she said slowly, 'is such a fan of yours he's not exactly an unbiased observer.'

'Good,' he replied as they took the flyover to Tullamarine airport. 'Perhaps some of it will rub off on his mother.'

And at the airport he made very sure he would leave an impression on her that would be hard to shake. In full view, he kissed her goodbye extremely passionately—so much so, she was shaken to the core and had to cling to him for a few moments while her breathing subsided and her knees stopped wobbling.

'Brett,' she breathed, her eyes huge and wondering.

'That has to last for two days so I thought I better make it double strength.'

She looked around and turned pink. 'But everyone's watching.'

'Let them.' He took her face in his hands. 'Now, promise me, no strange fancies while I'm not there to…keep all the tough times at bay. I won't let you go until you do promise.'

'My flight…'

'You'll just have to miss it.'

'I can't!'

He shrugged.

Ellie closed her eyes and breathed deeply. 'All right, I promise.'

'Thank you.' This time he kissed her very gently. 'See you soon.'

CHAPTER NINE

ELLIE got home without incident just as Simon got home from school and was treated to a most enthusiastic welcome.

So enthusiastic she asked him if everything was all right.

He screwed up his face. 'I've found out it's OK to be the one going away but not so hot to be the one sitting at home.'

Ellie laughed and hugged him. 'I know what you mean—hey, look at this!' And she produced the two Melbourne Cup caps.

Simon was immediately filled with awe. 'Bloody hell! I mean—holy moly, Mum! Martie and I will be the only guys in the whole school with these caps. You're brilliant!'

'My pleasure.'

'So you had a good time? Where's Brett?'

She described Cup day for him and explained about Brett. Then she paused and was about to test his reaction to the idea of her marrying Brett but something held her back.

Simon didn't notice the hesitation, though, and, apparently completely restored, asked if he could take Martie's cap over to him right there and then.

'Sure.' She ruffled his hair and watched him scoot out of the back door with affectionate eyes.

*   *   *

To her surprise, Gemma Arden came to call that evening after Simon was in bed.

'This is a surprise, Gemma,' she said as she answered the door. 'I thought our lunch date was next Monday.'

'I know.' Gemma plunked a heavy briefcase down beside her and fanned herself vigorously; it was a hot humid evening. 'But I have to go to Sydney on Monday and I felt so bad about postponing lunch yet again, I thought I'd call in on the off chance that you were here. I know Brett's not. He rang me about some business from Melbourne this morning.'

'Oh. Well, it's great to see you anyway! Come out onto the terrace, I've just made a jug of orange, mango and passion-fruit juice. It's very cold.'

'Glory be, you're a life saver, Ellie!'

Gemma was a big girl and, as always when she was working, clad in black and white. A long loose black jacket and skirt, white blouse and black-framed glasses. But she had a pretty face and long blonde hair, and over the years Ellie had come to know her as a shrewd, straight-talker with a rather acerbic wit that was refreshing.

'So,' Gemma said with a frosted glass of juice in her hand, 'how's Brett now? Still got those strange ideas you mentioned at the party?'

Ellie hesitated and suddenly knew the time had gone when she could discuss her relationship with Brett with Gemma. 'Well, I'm sure he was having difficulty readjusting,' she said slowly. 'Complicated by the presence of a topless dancer in his life.'

'Come again?' Gemma blinked several times and took her glasses off.

Ellie explained about Chantal and they laughed together for a bit.

Gemma polished her glasses and put them back on. 'I believe he's moved in here with you and Simon?'

'Yes—that was another problem. He feels at home here with us.'

'*Is* that a problem?' Gemma enquired.

'Well, no. It is his house. What I meant was, I assumed he'd either want his house back or we'd go back to the previous arrangement. I didn't imagine he'd be happy to live with us.' She shrugged. 'So I realized he was lonely and dislocated.'

Gemma thought for a bit. 'Of course it could all be to do with Simon. I think Brett used to feel quite useless when Simon was a baby.'

Ellie frowned. 'But he did so much for us.'

'Financially, yes. But now that Simon is older, and very much like Tom, I gather—well, it's probably all come back to him although time and again I've tried to tell him it was never his fault.'

'What?'

Gemma hesitated, as if suddenly sensing she'd stepped into quicksand.

'Gemma, Simon is my son and Tom was his father. Not only that but for years I've felt like Cinderella to Brett's Prince Charming, in a financial way at least, but I've always told myself it was because Tom was almost like a younger brother to Brett. Is there another reason?'

Gemma sighed.

'Don't you think I deserve to know the full story?' Ellie asked.

Still Gemma hesitated, then she came to a decision. 'Yes. He always felt responsible for Tom's death.'

Ellie's mouth fell open and she paled. 'But he wasn't even playing that day,' she whispered. 'That can't be true!'

'You may not know this but he has never played polo again from that day to this. And he was supposed to play that day but he had to pull out at the last minute and Tom, who was only a reserve, came into the team against an opposition he wasn't quite up to.'

Ellie's mind roamed back to that awful day but she hadn't been at the match either. 'He seriously thinks that?' she asked, stunned. 'How do you know?'

'Forgive me, but when he came to me to talk about setting things up for you and Simon, I told him I hoped he had a very good reason for embroiling himself with a woman he barely knew. That's when he told me.'

Ellie had a sudden mental image of Brett at the Melbourne Cup and the way his expression had changed when she'd brought up polo...

She released a slow breath. 'So that explains it.'

'Does it make it better or worse?' Gemma asked straightly. 'I don't know whether I should have told you but since I have—because it goes against the grain with me to think of any woman playing Cinderella to any man—how do you feel about it?'

Ellie tried to compose her thoughts. 'As if the missing piece of the puzzle has finally fallen into place.'

'On the other hand,' Gemma said thoughtfully, 'it struck me at Delia and Archie's party that you and Brett make quite a couple. And that things may have changed from his—original thoughts on the matter.'

Ellie smiled but said nothing.

Once again Gemma hesitated, then she steered the conversation to the mundane and finally she left.

Ellie barely slept that night.

It must have shown on her face because Simon asked her if she was OK the next morning.

'Just a headache—too much gallivanting around the country, probably.' She smiled at him. 'How are the rehearsals going?' The play was the next evening.

'Pretty good, but don't get too excited about my part, Mum. It's not a big one. They probably wouldn't even miss me if I stayed home.'

Ellie smiled and presently waved him off to school. Then she sat down and dropped her head into her hands. This is not a strange fancy, she told herself. This is the truth at last and I don't think I can bear it…

She got up and wondered briefly how she could dismantle eleven years in a few hours. But she squared her shoulders, poured herself a cup of coffee and set to work.

Two hours later she was in Simon's bedroom surrounded by partly packed boxes when she heard a car in the driveway. I'll just pretend I'm not home to whoever it is, she decided, and went on packing.

But whoever it was unlocked the front door with his own key and she stood like a trapped rabbit until Brett found her in Simon's room.

'So,' he said harshly, throwing his keys onto the bed, 'this is how little you believe in me, Elvira Madigan. Either that or you're extraordinarily well named.'

He wore a dark suit and a tie and she'd never seen him look more imposing—or harder.

'What's that supposed to mean?' she asked through stiff lips, unaware that she was as pale as paper.

'Hell-bent on tragedy,' he supplied and looked around. 'Prepared to uproot a kid to heaven knows where at a moment's notice. What about the school play? What about the kennel—how are you planning to explain it all to Simon?'

'Brett—' she dashed at some angry tears '—why are

you here? You weren't supposed to arrive until to-morrow.'

'I'm here because Gemma got in touch to tell me her famous habit of calling a spade a spade might have back-fired. Where did you plan on going, incidentally?'

Ellie swallowed several times. 'There's no "did" about it, Brett, I *am* going. To my father's for the time being—he and Simon get on like a house on fire. And this is for you.' She drew a piece of paper out of the pocket of her gingham dress, a cheque, and handed it to him.

He glanced at it contemptuously and immediately tore it up. 'Didn't the last few days mean anything to you, Ellie?'

'Brett...' she cleared her throat '...yes. And it so happens I was prepared to marry you even though I strongly suspect you'll be slipping off to Africa from time to time; even though your parents' marriage might have left a bitter taste in your mouth and made you something of a loner. But I will *not* be forced into a marriage with you out of a sense of guilt over Tom!'

'Ellie...' He stared at her.

'Gemma may feel she's backfired but she doesn't usually pass on disinformation.'

'No,' he said slowly and his shoulders slumped suddenly.

'So it's true?' she whispered.

'It's true that if I hadn't pulled out of the match that day it mightn't have happened. It's true that...' he paused and she noticed lines scored beside his mouth she'd never seen before '...Simon reminds me so much of Tom. It is not true that I've ever kissed you or made love to you with a sense of guilt in my heart. It just doesn't work that way.'

She turned away. 'But the whole concept of anything between us is flawed, it always was and it always has to be—the only difference is that now I know why.'

He put his hand on her shoulder and turned her back to him. 'Did things feel flawed between us at Peppers?'

Her breath caught in her throat. 'Brett,' she said with an effort, 'I wouldn't put too much credence on what happened in Melbourne. Something about being away from home, needing a break perhaps, a wonderful day— I don't know, it all went to my head.'

'You tried to tell me that once before—why don't we really deal in the truth, Ellie?'

Her eyes widened.

'I'll go first if you like,' he said, and took her hand. 'Come.'

She resisted for a moment, then allowed him to lead her into the kitchen. There was a pot of coffee on the stove and he heated it up while Ellie cleared the table of its usual paraphernalia and sat down.

'I was right about it being hot at home,' he said ruefully as he pulled off his tie and shrugged off his jacket.

Ellie didn't smile—she couldn't.

He watched her for a moment, then turned back to the stove as the coffee bubbled.

Presently he set two mugs on the table and sat down, and without preamble he said, 'You told me once you didn't think it could ever happen for you the way it had with Tom—falling in love.'

Ellie opened her mouth but closed it immediately.

'I wouldn't ever want to supplant that, or…erase it. And Simon, and what you feel for him, is living proof of it. The ultimate tie to a man you told me about yourself once.'

She made a strange, husky little sound in her throat.

'But this is what happened to me,' he said very quietly. 'Yes, there was guilt involved at first and I will probably always regret what happened. But falling in love with you, Ellie, was an entirely different matter. That spark you first aroused in me all those years ago fanned and grew without me realizing it at first.'

'How?'

'Little things. How you make and fly kites, how you love to cook, your voice, your hair, your skin, your sense of humour... Then I realized I always looked forward to coming home to this place.' He looked around. 'And how it irritated me not to be coming home to you in the true sense. And I found myself making suggestions out of the blue and realizing, a little to my amazement, that I meant them.'

He paused. 'Ellie, I know you can cite eleven years, Africa, Chantal Jones—it was none of that, it was you. But there was always, at the back of my mind, Tom's shadow. Not the guilt but the fear that you didn't ever want to love again.'

Her lips parted but no sound came.

'I don't know if you remember but I once asked you if you were expecting a declaration of undying love from me—you very quickly knocked that on the head.'

'I didn't...I thought...' Her eyes widened as she remembered that feeling of dangerous ground his question had aroused but also the sense of mystery.

'You thought I was mocking the idea? I wasn't. If anything it was a form of self-mockery—I got the answer I expected but wasn't hoping for.'

'I...didn't realize.'

'So,' he went on, 'when I had a fair intimation that it had to be you and no one else for me I have to admit I...used Simon and what I could do for him as a form of pressure on you. It was—' he shrugged, looking suddenly tired and unhappy '—blackmail pure and simple. But I couldn't help myself.'

'Brett...'

He put his hand over hers. 'If you've been wondering why I haven't even during and after Melbourne... burdened you with undying declarations of love, it's not because I haven't wanted to. I suppose I've been scared witless about what I might hear in return.'

She found her voice at last. 'I think I fell in love with you when you rescued me from that parking meter. I didn't know it at the time, or—I wouldn't admit it because it didn't seem possible. I suppose,' she said, with her voice clogged with emotion, 'I've felt guilty ever since.'

He went quite still and for a moment his eyes seemed to burn a hole through to her soul.

She waited with her heart beating like a drum.

He said her name on a breath, then he got up and drew her to her feet and into his arms. 'Thank heavens—'

'But don't you understand? It was only three months after I lost Tom.' Her eyes were anguished.

'Ellie, the point is, you *had* lost Tom.'

She stared into his eyes.

'Things don't stay the same, sweetheart. Things change in those circumstances.'

'Is that...is that what you meant about dealing in the truth?' she asked. 'Did you suspect all along?'

'No. I was hoping to get you to admit that you wouldn't sleep with any man the way you did with me unless you were in love with him.'

She was racked by the memory of their love-making and buried her head against his chest.

'Ellie?' His hands moved on her very gently.

She raised her head and her eyes were full of tears but she was smiling. 'No, I wouldn't.'

She felt the reaction in his body—a jolt of intense relief—then he was kissing her as if he were starved of her.

He lifted his head abruptly. 'How can I make up for all those years and for being such a blind fool?'

'Shall I show you?'

His gaze narrowed, then he nodded.

She took his hand and led him to her bedroom.

'I think I get the picture,' he murmured.

She laid his hand over her heart. 'Do you? I was going to suggest some wild, glorious sex but if you have any other ideas?'

'Not a one, my mind is a complete blank—that part of it that is not reeling from the thought of being wild and glorious in bed with you!'

They laughed together, then helped each other to undress with growing urgency. And the flame between them was more intense than it had ever been so that they lay in each other's arms speechless and shaken afterwards.

Until he said, 'About Africa.'

Ellie moved cautiously in his arms and kissed his shoulder softly. 'I do understand.'

'No, I don't think you do. I didn't understand myself until the other night when you fell asleep in my arms after I'd been talking about it. All of a sudden I felt different—yes, I'll always have great memories. Yes, one day I'd like to take you there.' He stroked her hair. 'But it's not in my blood any more. You've replaced it.'

She sat up. 'You don't have to say that.'

'It's true.' He cupped her breast. 'I always thought of

it with this…niggle of discontent because I wasn't there. Now I think of it with warmth and affection but the niggle has gone. As for being a loner, that has well and truly gone. I would have come home this morning anyway because I was missing you like hell.'

She sighed with sheer contentment and lay back in his arms.

'Happy?' he queried.

'Blissfully,' she conceded. 'And I know someone else who is going to be over the moon. You know—he missed me.'

'Why wouldn't he?' Brett asked.

She shrugged.

'You don't seem to understand what a special person you are, Ellie.' He rolled her onto her back and leant up on his elbow so he could look into her eyes.

'What can anyone say to that?' she answered ruefully.

'Then I see that I'll just have to remind you on a regular basis.'

'Oh, I wouldn't want you to have to work at it,' she protested.

'Work? That's a strange name for pure pleasure,' he said quizzically, and kissed her to stop her laughing.

They told Simon as soon as he got home from school.

His reaction was pure Simon. 'Yippee!' He threw his cap in the air, hugged Ellie enthusiastically and shook Brett gleefully by the hand. Then he sobered. 'That's a big weight off my mind, guys! I was only saying to Martie yesterday how grown-ups like to make things awfully complicated.'

Ellie closed her mouth after a moment and said, 'You've been discussing this with Martie Webster?'

'Sure. He's my best friend. We'd even cooked up a

little plan.' He grinned mischievously. 'I'm really happy I don't have to go through with it!'

'What sort of plan?' Brett asked in a strangled kind of way.

'I was going to fall off my bike, not too seriously, just enough to get Mum in a tizz so you could comfort her and patch me up and...' he shrugged '...be a hero.'

With a perfectly straight face Brett turned to Ellie. 'Why didn't I think of that?'

But she was laughing helplessly although presently she said, 'Listen, you two, I just think I ought to issue a general warning. You have ganged up on me in the past—don't even consider it in the future!'

'We wouldn't do anything like that, would we, Simon?'

'Only when it's really necessary, Brett,' Simon returned gravely. 'Hey—' he sat down at the table '—we've got a wedding to plan!'

They got married two weeks later.

Ellie wore a simply styled white dress encrusted with tiny white voile flowers and she carried yellow rosebuds.

Simon and her father accompanied her down the aisle, Simon bursting with pride and happiness and wearing his first suit. And although her father left her at the altar, Simon stayed at her side throughout the ceremony. After Brett had kissed the bride, he threw his arms around his mother and whispered into her ear, 'You did good, mon!'

The reception was small but lively—the McKinnons, Gemma Arden, the Webster family and her father and stepmother. And Chantal and Dan Dawson.

Chantal looked sensational. She was poured into an aquamarine silk dress and wore a cartwheel hat smothered in feathers. And she too, as she hugged Ellie, said, 'You did good, honey!'

Ellie laughed and thanked her, adding, 'How goes it with you and Dan?'

Chantal glanced over her shoulder to where Dan was standing beside Brett. 'You know, there's a lot more to Dan Dawson than meets the eye. Not that I've made any decisions! But he's getting to be a bit like a fixture in my life.'

Ellie squeezed her hand warmly. 'I'm—'

'Don't say it,' Chantal warned. 'But I'll keep you posted.'

After the reception, Brett took her away to a hotel for the night—they were to fly to Tahiti for their honeymoon the next day. Simon was staying with her parents.

Still in her slim, lovely dress, she waited while Brett tipped the bell hop. Then he came to stand in front of her and he took her roses and laid them on the bed and put his hands around her waist.

'You're looking very serious, Mrs Spencer.'

'That's because I'm seriously in love with you, Mr Spencer,' she replied, and added softly, 'Thank you for a lovely day.'

He drew her closer. 'I can see this is one of those occasions when I need to remind you how special you are—if any thanks are due for a lovely day, they're due to you, my darling.'

'Maybe it's just—us,' she suggested.

'You could be right. *We* are special.' He kissed her lingeringly.

'Although—' the little golden points in her eyes glinted at him '—you have done one thing for me that I'll be eternally grateful for.'

'What's that?'

Her lips curved into a gorgeous smile. 'I'm no longer Elvira Madigan.'

'Oh—is that why you married me?'

'Of course! Didn't you guess?'

'So...' his hands moved up her back and he released her zip and eased her dress off her shoulders and down her body '...it had nothing to with this?' Her bra came off next and she stepped out of her dress, and he removed his hands.

'That's...wicked,' she breathed as he stared at her breasts.

'Wicked, wanton—ah, wonderful,' he said softly as her nipples peaked and he covered them with his palms and looked into her eyes. 'Could this be a prelude to the kind of wild and glorious sex you specialize in, Mrs Spencer?'

'Try me, sir.'

He did.

Eighteen months later the first note on the fridge said:

Dear Mum, now that Lucy is 3 months old can I start teaching her to talk? And walk? By the way, I don't think it's good 4 her 2 b in her own room, she can share mine if you and Brett are going 2 b so heartless about this.
Your loving son, Simon.

The second note read:

Simon, talking, yes, but, going on yourself, you didn't walk until you were about fifteen months old so it's probably too early for that. Thanks for the offer of your bedroom, dude! But she'll be fine in her own room, promise. And I really appreciate all your help, I don't know what I'd have done without you.

Your loving Mum.

P.S. Brett says thanks a million too! And just to show we mean it, there's a frozen pizza in the freezer with your name on it.

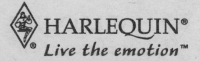

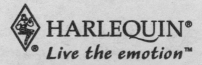

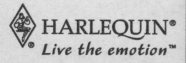

If you enjoyed what you just read,
then we've got an offer you can't resist!

Take 2 bestselling love stories FREE!

Plus get a FREE surprise gift!

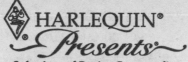

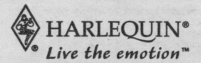

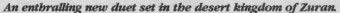

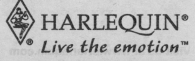

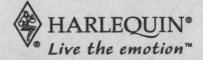